TREASON 3

TREASON

THREE
THE RISE OF THE LINAS

T. STYLES

NATIONAL BESTSELLING AUTHOR

2

By T. STYLES

ARE YOU ON OUR EMAIL LIST?

SIGN UP ON OUR WEBSITE

www.thecartelpublications.com

OR TEXT THE WORD: CARTELBOOKS TO

22828

FOR PRIZES, CONTESTS,

CHECK OUT OTHER TITLES BY THE CARTEL PUBLICATIONS

4

By T. STYLES

WWW.THECARTELPUBLICATIONS.COM

TREASON 3
THE RISE OF THE LINAS

By

T. STYLES

PUBLISHER'S NOTE:
This book is a work of fiction. Names,
characters, businesses,
Organizations, places, events and incidents
are the product of the
Author's imagination or are used fictionally.
Any resemblance of
Actual persons, living or dead, events, or
locales are entirely coincidental.

Library of Congress Control Number:
2022909717

ISBN 10: 1948373831

ISBN 13: 978-1948373838

Cover Design: BOOK SLUT CHICK

First Edition

Printed in the United States of America

What Up Famo,

It's been a minute, but we're back like we never left! The past few months have been insanely busy for us, but we couldn't wait to kick threw the doors with this one!

Our sexy blood suckers are here again! The masterful mind of T. Styles has weaved together a world full of mischief and drama worthy of the BIG SCREEN...or the SMALL SCREEN, just depends on how it needs to be seen.

TREASON 3 does NOT disappoint! Poor Cage, heavy is truly the head man, that's all I can say without saying too much! So, sit back and enjoy!

With that being said, keeping in line with tradition, we want to give respect to a vet, new trailblazer paving the way or pay homage to a favorite. In this novel, we would like to recognize:

TREVOR NOAH

Trevor Noah is a comedian from South Africa, a political commentator, a TV host, an actor, and author and soooo much more. Recently, our book club read his memoir, *Born A Crime* in which Trevor highlights pivotal moments in his life

By T. STYLES

growing up as a mixed-race boy with his tough as nails mother in South Africa during apartheid. The way in which Trevor depicts his stories was very captivating and at times, hilarious! Do yourself a favor, if you haven't already, grab this one, but listen to the audiobook version as you can hear Trevor tell you his story directly...Trust me!

Aight...T. Styles has unleashed the Wolves, so get to it!

See ya soon!
Charisse "C. Wash" Washington
Vice President
The Cartel Publications
www.thecartelpublications.com
www.facebook.com/publishercwash
Instagram: Publishercwash
www.twitter.com/cartelbooks
www.facebook.com/cartelpublications
www.theelitewritersacademy.com
Follow us on Instagram: Cartelpublications
#CartelPublications

#UrbanFiction

#PrayForCece

#Trevornoah

#TREASON3

By T. STYLES

Glossary

The Collective:

All Vampires

The Collection:

Vampire Groups

The Fluid:

Liquid Taken To Become A Vampire

Day Walkers:

Those Who Are Born With The Vampiric Gene But No
Fluid

PRESENT DAY

A soft breeze wafted over Violet's home and the moon sat high.

Due to a cloudless night, it casted a sweet glow. Inside Violet's residence, soft R&B music played. It was that classic shit that if you weren't careful could bring a baby into the world.

But that wasn't the case for Violet.

Instead of straight fuckin' she sat in front of her computer, staring at the ultraviolet rays emanating from the screen. The short strapped red dress she wore clung against her frame, showcasing her erect nipples and luscious curves. It wasn't the dress's fault.

She wasn't wearing anything underneath, to inspire the mood for the evening.

And then there was Pierre's fine ass.

On God, this man was fuckable.

Wearing a black shirt, which he left many buttons unlatched, he was revealing his chocolate chiseled physique underneath.

Why did the man have to be so fucking sexy? She thought, as he stood behind her smelling of sweet cinnamon and vanilla. It was such a strange mixture for a man that she wondered if it was deliberate.

By T. STYLES

Did he want her to devour him whole?

Because if that was the case, she would surely oblige and not leave a bite.

"The book is not going to write itself," Pierre said, massaging her shoulders. Her eyes closed as she became a victim to his touch. "You can do this, Violet. I have all the faith in the world."

"I would rather be doing something else." She turned her head and gazed upward at him. It was the type of look that let a man know she was open for his business.

"There will be time for that later."

She sighed. "Of course there will."

No matter what she did, it seemed as if she could never seduce him properly. Her efforts almost always ended up in vain, which ran contrary to the things he said in her ear on a repeated basis.

"I want you," he would say randomly while staring into her eyes. "Do you want me too?"

The moment she said yes, she would find herself in the same place she was now. In front of her computer being forced to pen a novel she didn't want to. Why was he so concerned with the characters in the story when they could be creating a world of their own?

"Then write, my sweet Violet." He would utter.

What kind of foreplay was that?

She looked up at him and back at the soft blue like screen. "I don't...I'm not sure if I can do it. My Abuela is a wordsmith and I..."

"You can and you *will*. Besides, your grandmother is dying. And she entrusted you with this job. Shouldn't you at least give it a fuckin' chance?"

She grew slightly annoyed. "How do you know I'm capable?" She whisked from up under his grasp and stood in the corner of the room. "You only just met me." Her arms crossed her body and sat right below her breasts. "But yet, you have all of this belief in me." She continued to stare at him from across the room. "That I...I..." she closed her eyes. When she reopened them, he was standing before her.

"Violet, stop this weak shit."

"How did you move so quickly?"

"Focus, Violet. On the book." His words were more of a demand, than a request.

She looked over at the screen from across the room as if it were a test, she was sure she would fail.

And then something happened in her spirit.

For a moment she hated her grandmother.

She hated how she entrusted her with such a heavy task that she wasn't built for. She wasn't a fucking

By T. STYLES

writer. She was only a girl. A woman in age but immature and inexperienced all the same.

Why would she think she would be able to finish her masterpiece without help? Which included weaving tales of love, lust, and betrayal.

Oh that's right? She was a fan who had been there from the beginning of the story's creation.

So if not her, then who?

Suddenly her eyes fell upon him.

He was wickedly handsome.

That's all she knew for sure.

But that wasn't enough anymore.

Despite the faint raised bruises on his face which healed with time he was alluring. The kind of man that could have a woman's soul without uttering one word. But again, why was he so fucking interested in her finishing this book?

"Who are you really?" She frowned, picking at her arm with soft pinches.

"I'm Pierre."

"Beyond your name. Who are you?"

For the first time she appeared to make him uneasy. And she liked it.

"This seems out of left field. Your soft attacks upon me. If you are unable to fulfill your grandmother's request, then say that. But don't question who I am when I've wanted to do nothing more than help."

"I get all of that. But why does your complete attention and focus hold me hostage? And then guide me toward that book!"

He moved closer, leaving no room between them. Carefully he wiped her hair behind her ears. She could feel him stiffen in his designer black slacks because he was sooooooo clooooose.

What was I just saying? She thought to herself.

"You're so fucking beautiful." His words interrupted her trivial thoughts.

Violet inhaled his sweetness. "No…no I'm not." She wanted more.

She could feel his attention would cost her and yet she was willing to pay the fee. From the moment she laid eyes on him she wanted to lay beside him instead. But he kept himself at a distance. Only fucking her in between requests for her to *finish the book*.

The book.

"My sweet Violet, You know I don't say or do things I don't mean. I'm also capable of dark things too."

It was true.

He was capable of many things.

But why was it aimed at her at the moment?

By T. STYLES

She thought about how he killed her sisters. To protect her after they jumped her to get at her money and possibly her grandmother's estate when she died. She even thought about how their deaths didn't bother her in the least. Maybe she was a monster too.

"What do you want from me?"

"Everything." His lips met hers and before she knew it, he picked her up. Her legs dangled along the side of his body.

Where had her panties gone?

Oh that's right. She wasn't wearing any because she was on some slut shit.

When did he enter her body?

He was so quick.

So thick.

It felt as if she was dreaming. Dreaming that all of this was unreal. But it wasn't. He was hitting that thang just right. Slowly he pumped in and out of her pussy. There was no need for foreplay. She had been waiting for this moment for so long, it felt like all her life.

The dick strokes felt as good as he looked.

Strong.

Sure.

Erotic.

While he moved in and out of her glistening pussy, she picked up on what could only be described as a hold back on his part. Every so often his head would drop alongside her neck. And he would angrily tilt it the other way, as if he were trying to prevent himself from doing some unknown act.

"What is it, Pierre?" She begged, as she had long since released an orgasm, while feeling herself on the verge of another. "What's wrong?"

"I don't…I don't wanna hurt you."

She was right.

He was holding back.

But why?

He was trying to prevent causing her harm, she felt. But instead of being afraid she looked at him, and with everything in her heart said, "Fuck up my life. Please. There's nothing you can do to me that I wouldn't beg you to do again. And again."

Slowly his head tilted in her direction, his mouth opened and then there was a ring at her door.

He moaned hard, releasing himself into her waiting body. "Fuuccccck!" He slammed a free palm against the wall. "Expecting company?" He asked, angrily.

"No…I'm…I'm not."

Slowly he put her on her feet and tucked himself back into his slacks.

She pulled down her dress and they both looked in the direction of the sound.

Whoever the visitor was, their presence was annoying at best.

But based on Pierre's huge mistake, also inevitable.

CHAPTER ONE
CAGE

The night sky was pitch black…

Some stars but not many filtered the scene…

No worries though…tall lamp posts dressed the tree lined street. Due to a recent snowstorm, the pavement was wet and shined like black diamonds. The lights that streamed downward gave a spotlight effect that lit up the block and glowed upon Cage and Onion who stepped into its radiance.

Cage Stryker, fine as aged wine tucked his hands into his black Prada raincoat while Onion, his frenemy, repositioned the collar of his chocolate fur coat for warmth.

From their locations, they looked around.

Searching.

They saw nothing.

"This is a fucking joke," Cage said under his breath.

"You the one that said it needed to be done." Onion looked from where he stood, around the block, peering intensely.

But Cage was so enraged his face crawled into a scowl. "She's unreliable…you can't trust her and–."

By T. STYLES

"You're still in love." Onion glared. "That's your first and last problem." He pointed his way.

Cage tried to put the anger back in the bag. But it was no use. Onion saw he was still moved by a woman he claimed to hate. "I don't know what you-."

"This is not about you," Onion said, stepping in front of him. "This is about-."

"Get out of my fucking face, nigga."

"Or what?" Onion said.

"Do you really wanna go there with me?" Cage stepped closer. Once friends, the two powerful vampires were sure to rip each other's throats out if things didn't simmer and soon.

"You need to give up any hope you have of being with her." Onion continued. "That's all I'm saying."

"And like I said, I'm not interested in anything but business. But even if I was there's not a fucking-."

"With time she won't remember you."

He shook his head and shrugged. "What does that mean? That she won't remember me?"

Silence.

"Onion, what does that-."

Suddenly a woman sang in the distance. They both paused, each looking around to find out where the sound originated from. The beautiful melody grew louder and higher as it continued.

And then it stopped suddenly.

Cage took a deep breath, closed his eyes, and focused on the air around him. His powers had been perfected in a way that made him, well, different. Unlike most vampires, he, and the Stryker Collection, those who took his Fluid in a ceremony, were far more advanced in their capabilities. Mainly because it was important for him that they always be practicing and perfecting so they did. It was known that most vampires had skills available to them that they had not honed.

Focusing harder on the air around him, slowly Cage's lids widened, and he looked upward.

There Angelina was, sitting on a lamp post, her feet dangling as if she were on a merry go round.

When he looked at other lamp posts, he saw the same. Various members of the Linas, her vampire Collection, who were just as beautiful as they were dangerous, all watching him.

"How did you get up there?" Onion asked, somewhat impressed.

She laughed. "Is that what you really want to know? After all, it's been years since the three of us have been *together*."

By T. STYLES

"Are you going to come down or not?" Cage said seriously.

"There he goes with that tone." Angelina said sarcastically. "I get the impression that he still believes he owns me."

"I never tried to own you."

"Good, because nobody owns my queen," a member of the Lina's said with authority.

"And if you were smart you would remember I am your king." Cage educated.

"We don't recognize you." Another Lina responded.

Tiring of the games, Cage positioned his legs to jump just as high, when suddenly growling from the shadows stopped his motions.

He couldn't see them, but he felt their presence.

"Ah, ah, ahn," Angelina said, wagging her finger. "I wouldn't do that if I were you."

Cage inhaled the air deeply. "Wolves."

The hidden growls were replaced with soft feminine laughter upon hearing his words.

"So it's true. You still choosing to keep time with outsiders." Onion yelled. "Fuck is wrong with you?"

She glared. "Where do I start? If I must-"

"If you came here to play games, why even accept the meeting?" Cage interrupted. "It's childish. Even for you."

"Because you're going to die tonight."

Mink, a member of the Wolves, stepped from the darkness.

"So you better have a good enough reason to change my fucking mind." Angelina laughed.

CHAPTER TWO
SIX MONTHS EARLIER

"Moon come through..." is what the stars appeared to say as they illuminated the night sky...

Below, in a pond swam the most beautiful vampires you'd ever seen. Completely naked, they enjoyed the moment to bask in nature since the early morning hours would never allow them to do so. In fact, any time spent in the sun would disfigure their frames, before eventually taking their lives.

The Stryker Collection laughed and played with one another while swimming and splashing water as their leader, Cage, looked at them from a slight distance. Their happiness, just the sound of their voices, put joy in his heart.

When he lost his mother and father and fell into an unfortunate beef with his siblings just because they were descendants of Wolves and he wasn't, he thought he'd never feel this type of joy again.

But he did.

They adored their king.

And he loved them. Hard.

The safety and peace Cage provided members of his Collection did something else. It caused Langley and Candy, two Strykers to fall in love. Even as they enjoyed nature, he saw them looking into each other's eyes, wanting to express more but being afraid Cage wouldn't accept their bond.

He couldn't accept it.

It was too dangerous to hear him tell it.

Still, he wanted the type of love that when you'd look at a woman, your dick would stiffen and your heart would pound, making it known that she was the one. But he didn't have it with Helena, his current girlfriend.

He wanted Angelina.

He wanted to go back to the past.

But nah. He had fucked that shit up when he isolated her and chose a woman he converted due to wanting someone who just like him, could no longer have the light.

Turning away from his Collection, Cage suddenly felt he was being watched. When he looked across the water, he saw a twenty-something-year-old man, with the word Daylight splattered across his yellow t-shirt looking in his direction.

He was a Norm.

And Cage could feel he hated him.

But why?

Suddenly the water swooshed softly as Helena, the new woman in his life, walked up behind him. She had taken The Fluid with forty-nine members of his Collection and had also taken him for herself.

But that bond was fading.

Placing her hands on his shoulders, water dripped down his tatted chiseled chest as the white gold and diamond pendant chain glistened.

"Hey, sexy," she said whispering in his ear.

"Bae."

She looked in the direction he was staring. Why does your heart call out to them? Do you know something I don't?"

"What you mean?"

"You know what I mean, master. Norms don't deserve our respect. They hate each other. Don't care about one another. If it wasn't for the blood that courses through their veins, they would serve no purpose."

There was so much she didn't know. So much he wanted to tell her and the rest of the vampire Collective. Like how vampires were put on earth to remind humans who they were. And how Wolves were in place to prevent the vampire population from growing out of control.

So Norms, as superficial as they were, needed to survive. But first they needed to evolve.

They needed to return to love.

He turned around and stared into her eyes. "Why are you filled with so much hatred all the time, shawty?" He wrapped his arms around her waist. "When it comes to Norms? We never talked about your past."

"You never asked." She looked downward.

"I'm asking now." He kissed her lips. "What could make a woman so beautiful be so cold?"

"You think it's cold to not care about humans?"

He glared. "I'm waiting." When it came to his Collection, when he asked a question, he always expected an answer.

"I have many reasons for feeling the way that I do, master. Our mere existence is made possible because the blood of those who don't know who they are, who are a weaker species in the first place, is intoxicating to us. And in case you haven't realized, very rarely do we walk past a human whose blood doesn't smell sweet."

"I'm still waiting on an answer. Why the hate?"

"It means they're all miserable. Worthy of nothing else but food."

"You want to be the queen? My queen?"

"I want nothing more."

28 **By T. STYLES**

"Then you must widen your view, Helena. Not just of the Collection but of life. One-sidedness doesn't give me the access I need to make informed decisions."

"I don't get–."

"If you're on my right I need you to have a fucking open mind. Not be so filled with hatred."

She nodded. "Is there something I should know about you and the humans? Because…because I feel you're holding back."

Silence.

"I know I hit you with too much already but let me say one more thing."

"Go."

"I know you used to bring Angelina here. I don't mind visiting your past, just as long as the same energy is placed in *our* future."

Suddenly Cage grew tense.

Someone was nearby.

Someone not there before.

Cage sniffed the air deeply.

There was a smell so clear that he knew immediately what was happening. And because he trained his Collection they also knew what was going on too.

All water splashing, swimming and jokes ceased.

Like a well-trained army they surrounded him for protection. And within seconds Row, Canelo and Shannon appeared from the woods. They wore gray sweatpants and no t-shirts which showcased their chiseled physiques. Tall in stature, their dreads rolled down their backs like snakes as they stood with authority staring down at the vampires in the water. Being of the Wolf bloodline, they brought with them a particular smell of wet dirt that was always alarming.

"Vampires taking night swims instead of putting on heirs in the club? Different." Row said readjusting his dick because it was so fucking heavy.

"Are you okay, master?" Langley asked, standing on his right, while also keeping an eye on Row and the gang. He was by all intents and purposes, Cage's muscle, who just like the other members of his Collection would protect him with their lives.

"And if he isn't?" Shannon growled.

"Then that would be a problem," Helena responded. "For you."

"I suggest y'all fall the fuck back," Canelo added.

"Or what?" Helena responded, fangs dropped.

The Wolves growled and the rest of the Stryker Collection dropped their fangs too.

"Everything is fine," Cage announced firmly, causing both sets to calm down. "Just give me five minutes." He exited the lake, the chain on his neck sparkled along with the water drops on his skin. Grabbing a dark green towel off a hanging branch, he dried his thick dick and wrapped it around his waist before approaching. "What do you want?"

"You know what we want."

Cage chuckled once. "I don't read dog mind."

They growled at the disrespect.

"Where's Bloom and Flow?" Canelo interrupted.

"You niggas don't listen." Cage said, shaking his head. "Like I told you a million fucking times, I don't know where they are. What part don't you get?"

Lies.

Cage knew exactly where they were.

After becoming a direct threat to vampires by lusting after their flesh, including his own, he had them snatched off the streets and placed in a renovated apartment underground. The land was used to provide a safe haven for Vamps in the event of an attack. And so, the conditions were far from unsavory, but it did mean removing all freedom.

"We don't believe you."

"I don't give a fuck what you believe." He shrugged.

Row stared at him a bit longer. "I respect you. I know you're a good man, despite being a vampire."

The Stryker Collection, wrapped in towels, stood even closer to their leader.

"But you need to know that Tatum's influence is getting stronger with the pack." Row continued.

"He's my brother. I wish for him greatness." He said honestly.

"If you knew what that meant you wouldn't be so cocky," Canelo added.

Cage chuckled once.

"Listen, Cage, can I talk to you in private?" Row pleaded.

"We were just-"

"Please, man."

Cage nodded and they stepped away from everyone.

"There's something else," Row started. "Before your father died, at one point in time, he ate vampire flesh."

Cage's eyes widened. "I...I didn't know. He never told me that. I always assumed he-."

"I'm sorry I thought you knew."

Cage dragged his hand down his face. "I knew he didn't want me around. But I thought it was just V and Wolf shit."

"It went deeper." Row continued. "We have always known or heard stories of this being possible. And that once a Wolf tastes vampire flesh, he craves it more. But lately these urges are coming up again in higher numbers with my people. And I don't know why. Do you know what's going on?"

Cage sighed. "Nah."

More lies.

Row nodded. "I hope what you're saying is true, because I feel like something is about to kick off. And as far as Bloom and Flow, if Tatum even thinks you're holding them against their will, I don't think blood will prevent a war from popping off. So for your benefit, and ours if you have them, turn them over. Please."

CHAPTER THREE
ANGELINA

I t was a beautiful night to ride…
Purple and black Ducati motorcycles zipped up and down the racetrack in a hurry. In the far back of the track was a high wall that was splattered with advertising sponsor logos.

Sexy ass vampires, with long flowing hair, thick thighs and fat asses handled the bikes with extreme speed as their leader, Angelina, stood with Mink, a beautiful Wolf who was once Flow's girlfriend. And Carmen, who was converted with Onion's Fluid and was the only remaining member of his original Collection.

Angelina was wearing a black leather biker catsuit that ripped at her curves. Her hair fell down in luscious curl locks over her shoulders. She had gotten finer with time. As she continued to observe her ladies racing, Angelina thought about her closest friends. Both Mink and Carmen held deep seated grudges and as a result had reasons for joining Angelina.

It made her uneasy.

By T. STYLES

For starters, Carmen was upset with Cage. Appreciating the fact that he was Tino's son, she hoped to be converted into his original Collection, believing his Fluid to be more powerful. But his rejection of her in public at a nightclub caused her great anger which she held onto even at the present.

Mink, on the other hand, had other reasons for joining the vampires. And it had everything to do with Wolf culture and their archaic beliefs. Once a female Wolf took a male Wolf sexually, she was considered used or washed up if that man ever abandoned her or disappeared. Considered trash, these women would be used solely for sexual purposes.

So when Flow went missing, Mink felt alone. Other female Wolves felt the same way for their own reasons. And so they joined Mink on her journey of revenge.

As the Vamps revved up and down the track, Angelina could feel Carmen and Mink's uneasiness.

Mink had almond-shaped eyes, light brown skin and beautiful locked hair that ran down the middle of her back. She was stacked in a way that was appealing to the male species with 'A' cup breasts, a tiny waist and a large ass that presented her body in an hourglass shape.

Carmen, on the other hand, had perfect opal colored skin with full pink pouting lips. Due to being a vampire, her shape filled out in ways that caused both men and women to do double takes when she switched by. She oozed sex appeal.

"Ladies, when you've finished on the bikes, work on your climbing skills on the back wall!" She yelled. "We must be quick and agile at all times!" She looked over at Carmen. "Spit out what the fuck you want to say. Your stares are annoying."

She looked down and back at her. "My mistress, when I came to your room last night, to talk to you, I saw you crying."

Angelina clutched her hands in front of herself. "You heard wrong."

"That's not true. It's been happening for a while. What's...what's going on? I just wanna help."

She wanted to tell her about Cage and how she still missed him after two years. She wanted to tell her how she got tired of fielding questions from her son, about his father.

Instead, she said, "Stop beating around the bush and tell me what this is really about. Because it has nothing to do with my tears."

Carmen nodded. "It seems like so much time is spent on trivial things lately."

Angelina whipped her long hair away. "Still you hesitate to say what's really on your mind even though you know I prefer otherwise."

Carmen looked at Mink and back at Angelina. "Angelina, what she's trying to-."

"Am I not your mistress too?" Angelina glared. "You being Wolf doesn't stop me from demanding the same respect. After all I feed you, make sure that you're safe. What's the difference?"

"There is none!" Mink admitted. "I just...I don't know. We want to speak about what brought us all together. But you get so angry that it makes it hard to bring up his name."

Cage was in the talk even though his name was not mentioned.

Angelina stopped and looked at Mink fully. "Continue."

"First I want to say I understand your pain." Mink resumed. "Not a day goes by that I don't think about Flow. But...but..."

"We had a plan, mistress. So why is Cage still alive?" Carmen interjected. "Because when we first got together the goal was to take out him and Onion. And yet they still move about like the world is theirs."

"Where's the glory you promised?" Mink asked.

"You and I both know you don't prefer glory." Angelina said. "You're after revenge, Mink."

"Aren't we all?" Carmen added.

They had clearly spoken at lengths and used the opportunity to attack her mentally together.

"If you both don't see the strides we've made, you're blind!"

"Perhaps if you made it clearer, mistress, I would understand. When are we going to put them out of their-."

"Mink, I don't have to make things clear for you! But you do have to trust me! Or does the Wolf DNA in your blood make it difficult for you to understand serious matters?"

The Linas paused what they were doing, after feeling their mistress' distress.

"You know, you claim to care about me, yet you use every opportunity to point out the difference," Mink said, on the verge of tears.

Over the months since they had spent time together, Angelina had seen her emotional side. Since her view of Wolves was always stereotypical...that they were strong and vicious, this difference shocked Angelina in the beginning.

Now she understood.

Mink was very emotional.

And Mink was always love.

"Mink, you know she cares about you the same way she cares about us," Carmen said, rubbing her shoulder. "You're the only person who knows where she sleeps at night. That shows the trust."

"And I am honored. But I still wish my voice could be heard. I wish what I wanted could be taken into consideration, seriously. This man...Cage...took the love of my life away from me. I don't have proof, but I know it in my heart. And I want him to pay."

Angelina took a deep breath.

Being a queen wreaked havoc on her soul.

And still, she was in charge.

Standing in front of her she said, "If I don't tell you how much I appreciate your loyalty let me start now. You didn't have to join me. I realize the bravery that it took for you and your Minks. Although we both have limited knowledge of the Wolves and vampire history, we can agree that based on our circumstances we shouldn't be friends. Yet we are more than that. We're family."

Mink nodded her head.

"But I also need to say this firmly."

"I'm listening, my queen."

"Just because you don't see the blueprint, doesn't mean the building won't be made. I have plans. Plans that will get revenge for you and me. But anybody can commit murder. I want more."

They both nodded again.

"Like what?" Carmen questioned.

Angelina sighed. "As we all know, for whatever reason Cage was selected to rule over the vampire Collective. So, I want to make things difficult for him. I want to cause dissension in his ranks and have him doubting if he has what's necessary to rule. And then I want the world to know of our existence so they can take their rightful place at our feet."

Mink smiled.

Carmen grinned.

"When he realizes everything he lost is because of me." She touched both of their shoulders. "Because of us...then we will take his and Onion's life."

"Do you promise?" Mink asked, finally understanding the grand plan.

"On my life. In the meantime, let's have fun!" She whistled until the Linas and Minks stood before her.

"That's enough practice! Let's go prepare! For tonight, we feast and fuck!"

Fangs dropped.

Wolves howled.

CHAPTER FOUR
OLD VAMP HALL

Nestled in a room inside a historic library, Viking, one of the vampire Elders, stood at the head of a huge mahogany boardroom table. To the right The Elders sat and to the left Cage posted up.

Alone.

The Elders had many questions.

"We see you've made quite a relationship with your Collection." Viking spoke before taking a seat. Over a thousand years old, he looked to be in his late thirties. "There are stories of how Day Walkers offer themselves to you, just to be a part of your Collection."

"I'm not converting anyone else right now. I can't deal with…with having to worry about…"

"Ones you care about?" Viking smiled. "I understand."

Cage sat back.

"While it is helpful that you are spending so much time on your own people, it doesn't move us any closer to the goal now does it?"

"Things take time." He widened the left and right side of his wine-colored suit jacket, exposing his black button down beneath. "You just have to wait." He adjusted the gold watch on his arm.

"Do we though?" He continued. "Or is it high time you start giving us what we want?"

"We're talking about people dying. Being sent to a battle, which would end in them being eaten by Wolves. This is not something I take lightly."

"I have a feeling that you fear death. But you shouldn't." He paused. "When a Wolf wants to die, he chooses the day, lets his family know and goes to a place of comfort and closes his eyes." He paused. "For us, it's the battle."

"What I'm doing will work. Because when people see how I take care of my own men then it will be easier to lead them to The Fringale. Plus I got several meetings scheduled with the heads of the largest Collections worldwide. I plan to-"

"Your ignorance is my fault." Viking continued.

"Fuck you just say to me, nigga?" Cage responded leaning forward.

"The Wolves are awakening, Cage. They're craving us as we speak. And if we are going to continue to exist you must lead a percentage of the vampire population to the slaughter. To the battle of The Fringale so—."

"I know all of this!"

"Do you?" Viking yelled. "Then why do you make us wait so long?!"

He heard this many times before and yet something about it felt wrong in his spirit. He realized that if the vampire population continued to thrive as it had then that would mean the end of humanity worldwide.

And at the same time what Helena said rang true.

Humans didn't give a fuck about each other.

So why should vampires?

Cage clasped his hands slowly before him and sat them on the table. Taking a deep breath he said, "I accepted the role you visited upon me. But I won't rush anything. You're going to have to give me more time."

"Cage, in about eight months the war will go down. Either you lead a percentage to the slaughter or we all die because Wolves will hunt us in droves. In clubs. In our homes. In our sleep. And I realize pushing my point may seem cold to you but this is our way." Viking continued.

"Seems to be that as long as you all lived, it shouldn't be."

"What does that mean?"

"Let me put it like this." Cage pointed at the table. "I got three objectives. First to prevent vampires and Wolves from knowing about The Cravings. I don't want mass hysteria. Second, to make sure Norms don't know we exist before it's time. Finally, to lead a percentage to the battle with the Wolves like you desire. So instead of pressuring me, just know that I am focused."

"Son, you are on the right track." Marco, another Elder said. "But we need a more specific plan. Luckily for you we've thought of it. This is what you gonna do..."

"This nigga here," Cage said under his breath.

"Excuse me?" Viking said.

"Go 'head."

Marco continued. "You will tell the vampires that due to some recent events; the vampires need to show up on the night of your choosing, at Fringale Park. If you hype them up enough, they will show up for unity. When they do, the Wolves will smell their scent, and kill them. Once properly fed, The Cravings will go away in a few months and everything will go back to normal."

"And of course because you are spearheading everything, this means you and your own Collection would be safe."

"You think that makes me feel better? That it doesn't have to mean my own people." He slammed his fist on the table. "The fact that it has to be any Vamp is tearing me apart."

Viking smiled. "That's what makes you the right man for this job. You care about them. You care about us."

Cage glared.

"Before you leave, Angelina and her Linas are causing a danger. If need be, are you comfortable enough to have her killed?"

"It's complicated."

"Are you comfortable or not?"

"I gave my answer. I won't make another."

Viking sighed. "You're dismissed."

After the meeting Cage abruptly exited the hall.

He knew it was treason to lead his own people to their death and at the same time he understood the need for population control. Being half human and half vampire didn't stop the guilt he felt from welling up in his heart.

How he wished someone else could make the decision.

How he wished someone else could determine their fate.

But wishing wouldn't bring him out of the situation. He was chosen. And he would have to rise whether he wanted to or not.

Once outside, the cool night air caressed his face. He was halfway to his car in the parking lot when he looked for his keys. He tapped his slacks, the left side of his blazer and the right.

Nothing.

"Fuck."

Rushing back inside, he doubled back down to the hall. Walking towards the door he paused when he heard Viking and Marco talking quietly.

He decided to eavesdrop.

"Every one hundred years we're blessed with a person like Cage," Viking boasted. "It was cutting it close this time though."

Cage frowned. What were they talking about?

"He will do what's necessary because he was raised by Wolves." Marco said. "And Wolves, whether they realize it or not, always have a sense of duty."

"True, I'm glad he's going for it," Viking laughed. "Because I was going to hit up his arch nemesis."

"Onion's too sloppy. It would not have worked." Marco admitted.

"True." Viking sighed deeply. "Let's just hope he doesn't get back on good terms with Onion and Cheddar and they tell him the truth."

"Anderson's disloyal ass really did fuck us over this time. He'll pay in the end though. I'll see to it."

By T. STYLES

CHAPTER FIVE
ANGELINA

A sexy ass Subterfuge Party was underway…

These parties were a way for vampires, who were already alluring, to entice Norms to the location in an effort to drink directly from the source.

Their necks.

Based on Vamp culture, it was against the rules to indulge this way. But the Vamps had long since abandoned policy to do what they desired. The only rule as far as most Vamps cared was to never, ever get caught. Their reckless behavior was one of the reasons Cage was having difficulty ruling.

He had to get them under control.

But it would be easier said than done.

Of all the Collections, Onion's was the worst. And they were the ones hosting the party, even though he wasn't in the building.

Using the art of seduction, which was close to being hypnotized, Vamps had a 100% rate of getting what they wanted. But the Subterfuge parties provided a trap. A private place for them to suck and fuck in seclusion.

When the Linas arrived, Angelina stepped into the party first.

Her hair rolled down her shoulders and back in patterns that made her look angelic. Wearing an Egyptian blue lace catsuit, she stood in the middle of the floor. Her Linas, along with Mink and her Wolves, stood behind her.

Pussies clean.

Bodies sexy as fuck.

The moment she stepped inside; Norm men were weakened by her beauty. After all, being Vamp freshened the skin and thickened bodies in ways that appealed to the weaker species. In fact vampires evolved over time to include everything Norms valued. Beauty. Sex. Power.

"Wait, I thought this was Cage's spot," Carmen asked Angelina.

"Let it go," Mink said, already getting hungry. "We're here now. Might as well have fun."

The vampires were for the Minks.

And the Norms were for the Linas.

In the end Angelina's mob would have their way.

"I can't verify it, but Cage never allows his Collection to be in clubs." Angelina said, looking around while licking her lips. "So, Onion's people will have to do for tonight."

Donte' Drip Drop, who had received the invite from a Vamp, he had unknowingly befriended, walked toward her as she eye fucked him from afar. He heard from the Vamp who lured him there to be sucked on by members of his Collection, that the party would bring the baddest women.

So far he was right.

So when Donte' saw Angelina, he gripped his thickened dick, grabbed his drink from the wet bar and stared across the club at her.

She smelled him instantly.

With a fetish for Baltimore men, believing their blood tasted the sweetest, she ran her tongue across her teeth. She wouldn't drop fangs just yet, but she intended on sucking him dry before the night called upon the sun.

"Spread out, Linas," she directed, never taking her eyes off the man who eye fucked her from across the way. "And Mink..."

"Yes, queen."

"When we're done, you and your Minks can feast on V."

Mink nodded. "Got it, sexy."

Slowly she sauntered toward Drip Drop. She saw him catching every one of her curves and knew he couldn't resist. She dipped and raised her hips until she stood before him in all her splendor. "You see something you like, big boy?"

"Big boy, huh? I haven't heard that term used since I was a kid."

She giggled. "But you heard it all the same."

"I'm a grown ass man." He repositioned his dick. "Can't you tell?"

"I was talking about this…" She gripped the bulge between his legs.

"Whoa. I knew you were fine. But bold too?"

When the song that spoke to both of their souls boomed from the speakers, he wrapped his arm around her waist and pulled her closer. She didn't struggle. Instead she gave him the honor.

All was fair in blood and war.

Glancing around the club she saw the Linas doing the same thing. Each of them had a man of their choosing who would be completely drained before the night ended. And if they smelled as sweet as he did she reasoned they would be full off blood for the next couple of days. That wouldn't stop them from sucking again just for the pleasure and the fun in the future.

"What's your name?" He asked, as if he was in control.

"Angelina."

"A pretty name to go with that pretty face. I'll take it."

"I want you to take a little bit more than that."

He chuckled once. "Is that right?" He looked at her closer. "Who let you get away? I mean, you fine as fuck. Say what's on your mind."

"My pussy was wet when I first walked over here but now you talk too much."

"My bad."

"Do you have a chamber?"

A chamber was a space within the party that was dedicated for privacy. Newcomers who were basically Norm's thought the rooms would allow them to fuck in private. What they were actually used for, however, was a place to feast from the source for vampires.

"Yeah." He gripped her closer, liquor stemming from his breath. "Didn't know what a chamber was for at first but my man assured me I needed one." He breathed her in again. "He was right."

She grew serious. "Are you inviting me into your space with you?"

"Fuck you think?"

"I need you to say the words." She said firmly.

"Yes."

"Take me there."

The moment they entered the small but just big enough sized room, she shoved him down on the cushioned bench style seating. Standing in front of him she removed her catsuit as if it were holding her back.

Now undressed, she stood before the man completely naked.

Nipples perky. Waist small. Ass fat. Hips rounded.

She grabbed at the right side of her hair and allowed it to drape across one breast, leaving the other free.

He had never in his fucking life seen a woman that fine. He tried to spot a flaw on her body to at least be able to take her down from the high horse he was sure she was on.

But she was sheer and utter perfection.

Living breathing art.

Walking toward him she stood on the bench that held his body. Positioning her pussy in front of his face she said, "Lick, nigga."

He couldn't do it fast enough.

His tongue softly flipped her button repeatedly until it glistened like a wet pearl. Within seconds his tongue became a ladle, entering her tunnel with precision before bringing the juices to her clit again.

Angelina loved getting her pussy sucked before she drank from the source. So this was right up her alley. Grabbing the back of his head with both hands, she grinded against his mouth until her fangs dropped due to the lovely sensation that coursed through her body. Luckily for her he had been stroking his dick to a completion because she wanted that thang next.

Juicy wet, she eased on top of it until she covered him in full.

"Oh my...fucking...why do you...why do you feel so good?" He asked. "You so wet."

"You like this?"

"I love it."

"Good..." She looked into his eyes and her fangs dropped.

"What the fuck?" He was scared and turned on at the same time that he was struggling to understand what he was seeing. What was she? "How did you do that?"

He attempted to get from up under her but vampire strength was powerful. It was of no use.

"Easy, big boy," she said, continuing to buck her hips. "I'm glad it's juicy enough for you though. Because I'll be your last piece of ass."

Lowering her head, quickly she bit into his neck while bucking and popping like the baddest stripper. As her teeth marks sank deeper, he continued to fuck her until his arms fell alongside his body in weakness.

She grinded and flexed on the dick until she came once more, and he was dry. "East Baltimore niggas are the best."

When he was bloodless, she eased up and wiped her mouth with the back of her hands. Opening the door she yelled, "MINKS...FEAST!"

Within seconds Wolves grabbed the Vamp of their choice and ate happily, as Angelina and her crew officially made their presence known.

In a sense, it was the Linas coming out party.

If she had things her way, the world would finally know of the Vamp and Wolf presence. And they would also know who ran shit.

Bitches!

CHAPTER SIX
CAGE

In a 69 position, on the floor in their room, Cage sucked Helena's glistening pussy as she bobbed her head up and down on his dick. Stroking his balls while making his stick sparkle, he couldn't wait to press inside his lady.

She was doing that shit so well he was sure he would release his flood into her mouth, leaving her only partially satisfied. He wanted to beat at that box though.

"Get up here."

"No, you taste so…"

"Now!"

Obeying her master, she quickly did as told and eased on top of him. Her fingertips pressed down into the fibers of his chest as she raised up and slammed down repeatedly. He was just about to explode when Arabia opened the bedroom door ever so slightly. Something she had done before, which drove him insane but then she would claim it was an emergency.

Instead of getting angry this time, he allowed her to watch quietly from the slit.

He knew she secretly had a thing for him.

And if she hadn't gotten so sneaky and untrustworthy over the years, he would have laid the pipe and sucked on them fat titties while she called his name a long time ago for fun.

As charity of course.

But she couldn't be trusted and so she would have to resort to intrusive measures to get her rocks off.

"I'm cumming, baby." Helena said.

"Word?"

"Yes, I'm…I'm almost right there."

Hearing the passcode, Cage pumped one last time before he splashed into his girl. Just that quickly he was done. After they both reached ecstasy, she fell into him.

Slowly her lips met his as he gripped her ass cheeks and spread them gently. From Arabia's view she could see where his dick still connected to Helena's pink pussy, and so he widened it a bit more for her viewing pleasure.

Hating like shit, she rolled her eyes and closed the door, causing Cage to laugh.

"Why do you do that woman like that?" She said, kissing his lips once more. "You gonna give her a heart attack." She eased up slowly, and his dick fell on his stomach.

"How you know what I was doing?" He grinned.

By T. STYLES

"I can read your mind when you leave it open. I also know you were thinking of Angelina again."

He got up.

She was about to fuck up the entire night.

It was exhausting sometimes to remember to leave his thoughts closed. Because if he didn't, Helena would pick through his mind for thoughts of his ex-wife.

"You know what...let me get dressed."

"No response?"

"None needed. You know everything, remember?" He moved toward the bathroom. After taking a shower together he threw on his robe and walked into his lounge where Arabia was waiting.

On his table sat a huge box of black golf balls and he placed them on the floor.

Going to his refrigerator he removed a cup of blood to quench his thirst. Her eyes remained on him the entire time.

She was sitting on one of the recliners all tight faced. Her red glasses were steaming. He also saw a balled-up piece of tissue in her hand and knew she used it to wipe herself.

He could smell it from across the room.

"That was rude, Cage."

"Which part? You entering my room without waiting for me to say come? Or the fact that you were so wet you had to wipe yourself?"

"You don't know what you're talking about."

He laughed. "Yeah aight. If you would stop violating my privacy, you wouldn't have to shower later. Now what do you want?"

She looked down and back at him. "What's with the balls?"

"It startles distracted vampires."

"I don't get it."

"What do you want?"

She cleared her throat. "Something is happening that I foresaw and unfortunately you have to address."

"One of these days you'll tell me what you want straight up instead of beating around the bush. It's one of the reasons we can't get along." He took his seat and adjusted his chain. "Now what do you need?"

"Angelina and her Linas made a scene at a Subterfuge party."

"Who hosted a Subterfuge party against Vamp policy?"

"You and I both know Subterfuge parties are a regular. Especially in Maryland. But they've been going on since the beginning of time. Most go off without a hitch. But this one was particularly violent."

"Drinking from the source. To death. Sounds like nothing new."

"That and the eating of vampires."

Cage's blood ran cold. He leaned forward. "What are you talking about…eating of vampires? Vamps don't eat other Vamps." He knew that Wolves did, but up until this point it was only done in small pockets.

"From the one vampire who was able to escape I discovered that Angelina is in the company of female Wolves. And they must have some understanding because why else would she stand by and witness her own people be slaughtered?"

Cage rose slowly. "Do Norms know about this party? Did it make the news or any other media outlet? And do Wolves know what's happening?"

"I don't think so."

"Good."

"Well…not really."

"Explain."

"There is this influencer named Dickens. He's been trying to convince people for years that vampires exist, after he claimed his mother was turned and tried to bite him one night. He hasn't seen her since. And so he's motivated to cause us problems."

"Is it gaining traction?"

"No...but if they catch a video one night it will." She paused. "When the vampire escaped, we went in and did what we had to do to clean it up. But The Elders are upset. Because so many vampires died last night, there was a lot of pain for those in their Fluid line. Many are still recuperating."

"Fucking Onion converts a bunch of niggas and don't tame 'em! Allowing them to be plucked off like low hanging fruit? What is wrong with this dude?"

"Angelina is wrong with him. Angelina is wrong for you too."

He smacked at the air. "This...I don't think she could do this. Where would the Wolves come from?"

"It is her!" She yelled.

"Arabia, lower your voice." He said calmly. "Don't let the fact that you saw my dick make you believe we're equals."

She swallowed the lump in her throat. "You know I didn't mean it that way." She looked down and then readjusted her red framed glasses. "But you know she's an addict. First drinking from the source produces effects that drinking from a cup could never provide.

But now she's hanging with Wolves. She won't go back to our way. She must be taken care of!"

He sat back in his chair. "Who else knows? Other than The Elders."

"The clean-up crew. And then I rushed here to tell you first."

"Don't tell anyone else, especially other Vamps. There have been only whispers of Wolves craving vampires. If this gets out it will be tragic. I'll take care of it."

"Cage, I-."

"I said I'll take care of it! Now go!"

She jumped up and stormed out.

Repositioning on the other side of the chair, using his mind he said, "Langley, come see me."

A minute later he was there. "Yes, master."

"I need you to find Onion and Cheddar. Their locations. Something has come up with Angelina I must handle but I need to speak to them too about what I overheard with The Elders."

"I'm on it. But...I wanted to talk to you about..."

"If you bringing up a relationship with Candy, that you know I forbid, I don't want to hear it."

"I'm sorry, sir. You're right. Let me fulfill your request." He rushed away.

Cage had seriously underestimated Angelina. He thought she was weak and a woman who could be overlooked.

He was wrong.

His dismissal of her feelings made her a problem. He needed to dispose of her as soon as possible. So why was his dick hard?

CHAPTER SEVEN
ONION

Onion with Cheddar at his left just closed on a new property big enough to operate as headquarters for his Collection. Since the plan was to dig underground, he was sure it would provide them safety in the event they had to escape. He had two hundred members of his Collection to be concerned with, but after the Subterfuge party that Angelina crashed, he lost twenty more.

Onion and Cheddar walked toward their cars after leaving the real estate agent. They remained silent until, "Are you going to say something or stand over there looking all stupid and shit?"

"Do you want to hear what I have to say?" Cheddar asked, posted up in front of him with his hands clutched.

Onion glared.

"Do you remember why I agreed to support you?" Cheddar continued.

Silence.

"I thought you would live up to what Tino saw in you. I thought you would be the leader of The Collective."

"Get to the point, Cheddar. Because we both know Cage is their fucking boy."

"Onion, you have to do a better job commanding your people. That party took out members of your Collection. Imagine if you weren't their leader. You would be down and in pain like many Vamps are tonight."

"But I am their leader so it doesn't apply to me."

"You have to tell them niggas to be careful where they go. They being hunted. We all are. At the end of the day there's no need for Subterfuge parties. You have access to blood. Feed your fucking Collection. They're young Vamps and they out here acting stupid."

"I never wanted the responsibility, remember? I told you I didn't feel like being no father."

Cheddar was heated. "Wow. They aren't your children. They're your army."

"I have something planned that's bigger than anything you can imagine. And it will undo a lot of things."

"Undo a lot of things? I'm not talking about fanciful thoughts, Onion. I'm talking about reality."

"And I am too! Trust me. I can literally control what happens." He glanced down at his watch. "Look, I got some place to be. We'll discuss this later. But trust me when I tell you I have things under control."

"Yeah, whatever."

Ten minutes later Onion parked in front of the abandoned restaurant. It shut down years earlier after a fire Onion set ravaged the property. Sponsored by Vamp Rage, he decided to act violently after waiting for Angelina to show her face one night.

She didn't.

Embarrassed that the staff and customers thought he was a gump for constantly showing up and being alone, he set gas to the spot and watched it light up the sky.

That was many years ago.

This was now.

Despite having no connection with Angelina after he used her pregnancy against Cage, and converted her to his line, he still showed up every night, hoping that she would forgive him for using her to get at Cage.

After all, despite her rage, he was still her master.

His Fluid coursed through her body.

Sitting on the curb, he was shocked when after a year, she finally showed up. Angelina took his breath away. She was so fine that for a moment he lost focus. She had always been bad but since being Vamp freshened her skin she looked like she stepped out of a magazine.

"It worked." He said to himself.

Walking up to him in a pair of tight jeans and a black top that cut low she smiled as if all was well with the world. "Onion."

"You look beautiful. I'm glad you let me see you again. Since I did convert you which makes me your master."

"You haven't seen me in over a year and that's all you have to say to me? After all, I did kill your Collection."

"You mean your family too?"

"They ain't no family of mine just because we all drank your cum."

He chuckled once. "They shouldn't have been there anyway. I'm over it."

"Wow...unlike Cage, you really don't give a fuck about your own people." She stuffed her hands in her pockets. "I'm not sure why I'm here either. After all, you destroyed my marriage. But he was never the man I thought he was anyway." She looked downward and then back at him. "But that's the past...I..."

"You still miss him?"

Silence.

"How you been, Onion?" She asked, ignoring the question.

He chuckled. "I'm good. Been thinking about you. Worrying about you. But it looks like you're getting enough blood."

She laughed. "I make do. Back to my point, you really should care for your Collection. How they operate in the world makes them my favorite victims for my Wolves."

"Everything will work out." He took a deep breath. "But...let me take care of you. Make sure you never go thirsty a day in your life."

"Take care of me huh?"

"I have never gotten over you, Angelina. You know that right?"

She stepped closer. "Do you really want me?"

"More than any fucking thing. But do you forgive me?"

She looked down and back at him. "If you really want me...if it's really true... take me with you now. I've been needing the touch of a man and..."

He stiffened in his jeans. "I hope this not a game."

"It's not. Show me how much you really miss me when we're alone."

He smiled widely but slowly it went away. "Hold up, are you trying to seduce me?"

"Seduction works on vampires too?" She said in a childish tone.

"You know that it does."

"Take me with you." She pressed harder. "Take me home."

Thirty minutes later after being blindfolded, she arrived at his crib and eventually in his bed. At the moment they were both fully dressed but it didn't mean the sexual tension wasn't at an all-time high.

He was lying face up and she laid in his arms like they did back in the day as teenagers. "I'm glad you wanted to come."

"Me too."

"But when I invited you over here, I didn't mean for you to be in my bed." He played with a strand of her hair. "I just wanted to spend the time."

"Onion, if I didn't want to be in your bed I wouldn't be. I'm not a little girl anymore. I don't need protection."

"If I could...if I could make you forget anything in life, what would it be?"

"What are we? Ten years-."

"I'm serious."

She thought about his question and Cage's face entered her mind. "I wish I never met Cage."

He smiled. "Are you sure about that?"

"More than anything." She took a deep breath. "But that's all pretend. Right now you talking too much." She rose up and pushed him backwards. Next she removed her jeans followed by her panties. She was moving so quickly, it was robotic.

But he was too excited to tell the difference.

After all, it was Angelina.

The one.

He wanted her so badly she could have laid still and still he would have fucked the shit out of her. Because there was no way he could resist the love of his life.

Suddenly the bedroom door flew open and Cheddar entered.

"What the fuck!" Onion yelled. "What are you doing in here!" He was still tucked inside her.

Cheddar grabbed Angelina by the hair, disconnecting their bodies.

"Get off of me!" She yelled, slapping at his hand.

"What are you doing?" Onion yelled, covering his dick. "You know how I feel about that woman! Do you wanna–."

"Look out of your window!"

"But we were—."

"Now!"

Grabbing his sheet, he covered himself before walking to the window. Scattered on his lawn like yellow dandelions were beautiful Wolves. Their hair hung down their backs but each one was coming ready to attack.

"What's going on?" Onion asked Angelina.

"You already know." She said slyly. "Can you get off my hair?" She yelled at Cheddar. "Please."

They were on their way to attack Onion, possibly gnawing him to death. And luckily, Cheddar's Collection members were guarding them with guns aimed in their direction. Although Wolves could heal quickly from bullet wounds, they still felt pain and more than anything the moon was full.

Which meant each would have died immediately if shot.

"You would...you would hurt me like this?" Onion asked Angelina.

She smiled. "Fuck do you think?"

"Get her out of here." Cheddar directed. "And make sure the others go too." He told a member of his Collection before passing her off.

"Right away master."

Onion plopped on the side of the bed.

When they were gone, Cheddar sat next to him. "What is it about that girl you can't let go of?"

Onion smiled.

"She was about to let them eat you and you think shit funny?" Cheddar persisted.

He shook his head. "She wasn't going to let anything happen to me."

"Didn't you see them bitches out there? They were ready to kill!"

"They weren't! Why else would she bring them when the moon was full? My plan is working. She will fall back in love. It's just a matter of time."

CHAPTER EIGHT
CAGE

Tucked in a museum in Washington, DC, Cage observed the signature piece in the exhibition. Langley, Helena and ten other members of his Collection stood in various places, pretending to be interested in the works of art.

They could give a fuck about them paintings though. Cage was the true focus of their eyes.

Run by Vamps, the museum was called Du Sang which meant blood in French.

Langley walked next to him. "I still haven't found Cheddar or Onion."

Cage nodded. "I figured as much."

"But I heard from an agent that Onion just purchased property below ground. He also gave me some additional info that I'll move on soon. So I'll try again later."

"Let me know what you find."

The moment Row, Canelo and Shannon stepped inside of the gallery, all of the Vamps, including those who were not with Cage hissed with hanging fangs. Per usual they were wearing gray sweats and today, t-shirts.

By T. STYLES

Whereas the vampires were dressed in designer labels.

The Wolves stopped at the door upon feeling the heat.

"I'll talk to you soon about it." Cage told Langley. "Give me room."

He nodded and stepped aside, although still very near his master.

When it seemed as if a fight would kick off, Cage raised his hand silencing them. That quickly, they returned to observing the paintings. But every last one of them was secretly paying attention to their master.

Row approached Cage, who was ogling a painting of the sun with a vampire facing it full on. "This is...hopeful," Row said, observing the work.

"Is it?" Cage looked at it a bit closer.

"I'm not into paintings but I love seeing depictions of the impossible." He laughed once. "Vampires are great at taking the time to create things so visceral."

"While Wolves can't sit quietly enough to do anything involving their brains." Cage joked.

Row took a deep breath. "I don't know why it's so tense in here." He looked at the Vamps who were staring back. "I'm not the one trying to kill you, despite this recent smell that seems to accompany you all lately being so delicious." He looked behind him and back at Cage.

"Careful, Row." Cage warned. "There have been quite a few stories going on lately about Wolves attacking vampires. Don't get caught up."

"Like I said, I'm not your enemy. It's your brother you should be careful about."

"Then you should remind him who I am."

"Where are Bloom and Flow, Cage? You can end all of this by letting us know."

"Here I was thinking you just wanted to see me."

"Cage, I–."

"I told you I don't know." He said firmly.

"Except you do." Row faced him. "What is the meaning of all of this shit? Taking them away. You know how we are about our people."

"No I don't. Explain it to me."

"Our very culture dictates that we roll in packs. And when a member of our pack is hurt or lost, it involves all of us." He placed a hand on his chest. "Do you really want the Wolves at your door?"

"I think you should be easy about threatening my master," Langley said, involving himself in the conversation.

"If I wage a threat, he'll know." Row said, as Shannon and Canelo walked behind him. "Right now I'm giving him the facts because for real, all we want is the truth."

"Then if he says he doesn't know where they are, why don't you believe him?" Helena asked in a soft voice.

The moment they saw her face, the Wolves looked away quickly. Where the Wolves had it in brawn, the Vamps had it in beauty and she was striking. It was also believed that although they were from two different bloodlines, that the Wolves could succumb to the seduction of a Vamp if they weren't careful.

"And you are?" Row asked, refusing to look at her face.

"You'll know her name if I give it," Cage said. "Focus your inquiries on me."

"Fair enough." Row nodded and wiped his dreads away. "Let me make it plain, Tatum is not playing games." He pressed his palms together. "He believes that in order for him to show the Wolf nation his power, his siblings must be at his side. And he's right."

"Why keep sending you if he wants to show power? Because when he's ready to talk to me I'm here." He raised his arms at his side. "I'm family too."

"He only wants his Wolf siblings."

"So because I'm of a different bloodline I shouldn't be considered family?"

"Cage, I've said it before, you're the one. For your people. Not ours."

He chuckled.

"I'm serious. Your people will come to realize how lucky they are to have you even if it's not seen now."

"We see it," Helena assured him.

"As well you should," Canelo interrupted. "But we know what's in our destiny too. And that means having Magnus' sons on the throne, free and in good health. So without Flow and Bloom, Tatum can't prosper."

"Let me ask you something." He shot a finger his way. "Where was this energy when you threw Flow out the pack?"

"Come again, nigga," Row growled.

"After it was made known that he tasted V flesh you didn't want to have anything to do with him. You were afraid, and you should've been, that his actions would spark a war."

"Hold up, is this your way of saying you do know where they are?" Canelo asked.

"I'm saying if you cared about his well-being you would have done something back then. But you kicked him out because you couldn't handle him."

"I'm not about to argue with you," Row said.

"Good, because you would lose," Langley added.

Cage raised his hand to silence him.

"I'm sorry, master."

Cage took a deep breath and stepped closer to Row. "I don't know where they are. But if he doesn't believe me, like I've already said, tell my brother to come see me. I'll be waiting."

Row looked at his brothers who were behind him. But when he turned to face Cage, they were gone. And the museum was empty.

"What the fuck?" Canelo said.

CHAPTER NINE
BLOOM & FLOW

The underground apartment was luxurious...

Bloom was brushing her hair while across the room, Flow did push-ups to stay in shape. The muscular definitions of his body had reached all-time highs and he was as chiseled and as strong as ever. His mission was clear, to never find himself in the position he was in where someone took him against his will.

"You should bathe more, Flow." She stroked her hair again. Her mane hung down her back and draped over her shoulder.

"What I do with my body is none of your fucking business."

She turned her nose up. "Actually, it is. You work out like you're about to run a marathon. You prefer to stay in the living room instead of your own room and your sweat seeps into the carpet and couch causing everything to stink so badly I want to throw up. So don't tell me it's none of my business."

"Instead of worrying about me, you need to worry about yourself. All you do is eat and–."

"I have less than five percent body fat." She announced. "So don't try that shit with me."

"Less than five percent is still body fat."

She laughed and stroked her hair a few more times with the brush. Looking through the mirror at him she said, "How much longer do you think he will make us stay here?"

"Why ask me something so broad?"

"I really wanna know your opinion."

He stood up, grabbed a towel, and dried his face. "What he did by sticking us away is unforgivable. But I was already on the outs with him."

"So that makes it better?"

"Never said that."

"Then what are you saying?"

"That I'm not surprised I'm here. But what did you do? We've been together forever, and you refuse to tell me the truth."

She looked away. "I can't talk about it."

"Why?"

"Because I'm embarrassed."

"Bloom, what happened?" He sat on a chair a few feet away from her.

"I...I don't know really. I mean...it all happened after the event that you went to with Onion and the others. At the club. You shouldn't have been hanging out with him but you were anyway. Which was stupid in the first place."

"So this my fault?"

"Just listen."

He nodded.

"I overheard from one of the female Wolves, who was there that night, that they ate vampire flesh."

Flow's eyes widened. "You heard about that?"

"You know about it too?"

"Yes, them bitches called me that night at the hotel because at the time, I was in charge of the packs. That's the reason the uncles put me out. And that's also the reason we should talk more while we're locked up here." He wiped his face again. "But that still doesn't explain why Cage did this to you."

"First off, I'm not sure it was really my fault. I–"

"What happened, Bloom?!"

She took a deep breath. "My friend, a Wolf, convinced me to eat Vamp flesh. I liked it a lot. Nah...fuck that, I loved it. To this day there is nothing more pleasing or delicious. For weeks we went on sprees after that shit. Most of the V's came from Onion's Collection because they are easy to lure away and unprotected. And others were unknowns."

"So you expect me to believe Cage locked you away for Onion's people? When he don't even fuck with him no more."

"No...he cares about himself though." She looked down. "Like you know me and my friend spent a lot of time at the house. With Cage. He trusted me. He trusted us, I think. But one morning I...I caught my friend at his room door during the daytime hours. She was preparing to hurt him I think."

"You think?" He was getting annoyed. "Come on, Bloom. Tell the truth."

"It was around 8:00 that morning and Cage was asleep. And Rue said, *'Onion is going to kill him. What if we put him out of his misery earlier.'* And I knew what she wanted to do."

"So you were gonna let this bitch eat your brother?"

"No...I got rid of her even though I understood why she couldn't help herself. Because the smell of his flesh didn't leave me, Flow. Like...every time he came around I found myself wanting to...wanting to..." she started crying. "Hurt him. What's wrong with me?"

Flow rushed up to her and held her in his arms. "This is not on you."

"You stink, get away," she cried, trying to feel the hurt by herself.

"Stop fighting me." He laughed. "I'm serious though. There is nothing wrong with you."

"How can you say that?" She looked up at him. "Just the possibility of hurting my brother drives me insane."

He separated from her and took his seat. "Listen to me." He gripped her hand. "Them niggas are hiding something."

"Who?"

"Every fucking body! There is a reason this is happening to us. When your girl Rue ate that Vamp, and I had a piece too, Row and them were pissed at me. I found out that pops craved Vamp flesh before. Which is why he ain't like being around Cage after he took The Fluid."

"So this is…natural?"

"This sensation we feel is happening in larger numbers. Row and them know about our father but I'm sure Cage knows the real reason." He paused. "Somebody has to tell us something. No more games."

"Look at where we are. How can we get answers locked away?"

"We won't be here long. If I know my brother he has a conscience. That's his weakness. Not only that, but the uncles won't tolerate us going missing much longer."

"You think they gonna press Cage? Just for us?"

"I remember when Row and them came to church one day, to connect with us, when father was alive and we were kids. They'll do the same for us. I'm positive. It's the Pack Mentality."

"What you think Cage doing now?"

"Probably chasing behind Angelina. Like always."

CHAPTER TEN

Cars zipped up and down the busy Baltimore street blasting music varieties.

Angelina, alone, walked down the block wearing a full-length black jacket, a white shirt buttoned down just above her cleavage, tight blue jeans, and red high heels. She was fuck bait for sure. Every man she passed looked at her, and she returned their gazes willingly.

But it wasn't her eyes she was using to choose *the one.*

She was using her nose.

When she spotted the one, due to his aroma, who was about twenty feet away, she waited until his eyes fell upon her. Then, as planned, she dropped the contents of her purse on the block, exposing her cleavage in the process.

Seeing the beauty in a vulnerable state, quickly he rushed to her aid.

The moment he was within her breathing room, he gave off the most delicious fragrance ever.

She had to fucking have him.

He lowered down and helped her place everything back into her purse, then he looked down at her. "I didn't take anything." He raised his hands jokingly.

86   By T. STYLES

She winked. "I believe you." He allowed the straps of her purse to fall at the crease of her arm.

"So…where are you heading at this time of night? You should be-."

"Can I taste you?" She said, practically begging with her eyes.

"What…what did you mean?"

"Can I taste you?" Being an addict made her not as tactful as more seasoned vampires. She began to look at Norms like food and not humans with feelings or emotions. If she could have taken him on the street in front of everybody she would have done that too.

For sure, her desperate behavior alarmed him. He was suddenly turned off and so he said, "Nah, I'm good."

When he turned to walk away, she grabbed his hand and tugged hard. Not after she caught him in her trap would she let him leave. It was time to put him in a trance with vampire seduction.

"Are you…are you sure?"

"I don't-."

"You can say yes. "

Staring at him intensely, suddenly his answer changed. "Yes." He nodded. "Yes you can."

Having gotten the approval, she grabbed him by the hand and led him toward an alley. When they were alone, she dropped her purse on the ground, and she pushed him next to two tin trash cans.

"What you doing?" He asked, still under her influence.

"Just...just wait."

Sliding one trash can to the left and then right of him, she kicked her shoes off and hopped on top of the lids with bare feet. This gave her a height advantage.

"What is happening? Why are..."

Dropping her fangs, she bit him softly on the neck before he could say another word. The moment the liquid ran down her throat, her pussy moistened. He tasted better than she imagined and she sucked harder and harder. The sensation she experienced by drinking this way gave her a feeling higher than any drug or legal narcotic.

It was pure ecstasy.

He was awake, but in limited pain due to the erotic tingling he was feeling. Before long the more blood she took, the more he became weak as Angelina refused to let up.

Suck.

Suckkkk.

By T. STYLES

SUCCCCKKK.

She was just about to drain him dry, when a black golf ball came flying down the alley, banging into one of the cans. Startled, she pulled her mouth away from his neck.

"Who is that?" She asked. "I said who are you?"

Silence.

When she tried to see where the sound originated, from where she stood, she couldn't see anyone. However, she was no fool. She knew she was not alone. Afraid of it being police, she jumped off the cans, grabbed her shoes and purse and ran away.

The man, still alive but shaken, dropped to the ground.

When she was gone Cage stepped from the shadows and up to him having just saved his mortal life. The stranger's eyes were slightly open. Dipping into his own pocket, he removed a pill, put it on the Norms tongue and said, "Swallow."

He did.

When it was gone, he said, "When you awaken, you will forget about this night. If you don't, and you choose to tell anyone, I will find you. And I will kill you. Do you understand?"

He nodded.

Cage rose, stood up and walked away.

On God, Angelina was getting on his fucking nerves!

It wasn't just that he still cared about her. It was also about that every time she or her Linas did something in public, The Elders would link them together. This would put him in a bind as he was forced to listen to hours of complaints on why she couldn't continue her behavior.

He hated this king shit.

In addition to cleaning up her mess when she didn't know he was looking, he had another problem brewing before his eyes.

Cage was sitting on his patio with a half-moon high in the sky listening to a recording of a young activist who spoke of the vampires and Wolves existing on his social media account.

Like Arabia told him earlier, his name was Dickens, and he was doing his level best to warn society of their existence. He was also the one he saw at the pond that night. Cage discovered he ran a group called Daylight who sought to kill vampires by dragging them into the sunlight to be fried alive.

He had yet to find proof, but Cage knew it was his dream. And the way Angelina was carrying on he knew it would be just a matter of time before he fulfilled his goal.

Although there were many comments calling him mad, Cage was concerned that at some point they would start to listen. Especially if Angelina continued to act recklessly.

With a thousand members and growing, Cage was shaken by their presence.

"Master, your brother is here." Helena said softly walking next to him, pulling him out of the video.

He took a deep breath and cut off the device. "Let him inside."

"You know I'll obey you, but I'm not going anywhere. There's something in his eyes that feels off. Langley feels the same way."

"I don't need protection."

"So you won't mind if we stay close. Just for the show." She nodded and walked away.

They were serious as a heart attack about keeping him safe. Unlike some Collection members who didn't have a bond with their masters. Like Angelina and Onion.

Two minutes later Tatum walked inside. With time his muscles filled out like all Wolves. And the boyish look in his eyes vanished. It was obvious that he was a leader.

Tatum stepped closer and looked at the moon, his hands clutched behind his back. "Row said you kept asking about me."

"Row also said you kept talking about me." Cage responded.

Tatum grinned. "Do you ever think of mother?"

"Are you seriously asking me if a day goes by where I don't think about our mom? Or dad?" Cage questioned.

He looked at him and glared. "I am."

Cage took a deep breath, dropped his phone in his pocket and stood next to him. "I loved mother. And I loved father too."

Tatum looked at the sparkling Magnus chain on his neck and laughed.

"The humor?" Cage questioned. "I'm not finding it."

"You think donning jewels honors our parents?"

"It's a constant reminder to me. I don't give a fuck about what you think or anybody else for that matter."

By T. STYLES

"A constant reminder of what? Your disloyalty?!" He growled.

Feeling the heat, every member of the Stryker Collection rushed outside, ready to help tear him apart with a nod of Cage's head. And it may have taken every one of them too, because without a weapon and a full moon, Wolves were just as dangerous as vampires.

"Don't touch my brother!" Cage warned his Collection. "Nobody move!"

"He makes us uneasy, master," Langley yelled. "He means you harm."

"I get that! But remain where you are!"

The Vamps settled down but stood on guard.

"I'm not disloyal, Tatum. And I like that you speak up for yourself. As a man I want nothing more. But I would caution you to watch your tongue."

"You think I'm scared of your Vamps?"

"YOU SHOULD BE FUCKING SCARED OF ME!" Cage shoved him across the patio and before he could get up, he was over top of his body. The blow caused the air to smack from his lungs making it difficult to breathe. "I love you, but I won't suffer your disrespect much longer."

"Can you get off of me?" Tatum asked, breathing heavily. He misjudged his brother's strength but he would never do it again. "Please."

"Do you understand me?" Cage repeated.

"Yes." Tatum said through clenched teeth. "Now get the fuck up."

Slowly Cage rose.

Tatum rose too.

Dusting himself off Tatum said, "I see we're beyond words."

"I agree."

"So let me be clear, brother. You will bring Bloom and Flow to me within fourteen days or...well..." he looked at the Stryker Collection and back at Cage. "...let's just say I hope you take them wherever you go. Because you'll need every one of them niggas to keep me from snapping your neck." He stormed off.

CHAPTER ELEVEN
CAGE

Cage stood in front of ten members of The Elders with his entire Stryker Collection behind him at the Lyric in Baltimore. They were backstage. It was a theater where performances were hosted like plays, orchestras and the like.

And every seat would be needed.

Tonight was huge.

Because although he was deemed king and had made an impression on The Collective as a whole, he had yet to give his plans for the future. Sure he was Tino's son, but at the end of the day he was raised by a Wolf. And so he had to be careful with his words as he tried to win them over.

While he waited to conduct his big speech, Viking kept running his mouth, making him uneasy.

"...and if you could start by telling them how important it is to look out for one another, especially since the Wolves are attacking us, things should work out. Don't mention The Cravings though. It will spark fear. Never, ever mention them in fact." He wagged a finger, sending Cage over the edge. "Next tell them about how the Wolves are offering us up to battle at The Fringale and–."

"I'm going to decide what to say to *my* people. Not you!"

Langley grinned, loving his master's firm stance.

Even Helena raised her head higher in pride.

"So you don't even want to hear what we have to say?"

"I didn't say that. But I'm the one who has to gain trust. Not you."

Despite respecting their leadership, Cage had no intentions of allowing them to use him as a puppet in a regime to manipulate The Collective. If he was going to win them over, he would do it his way.

"We have no doubt that you will know what to *say*," Marco chimed in. "The concern is if you know how to *lead*."

"He does a pretty good job if you ask me," Langley added.

"And yet you talk out of turn when I'm talking to your master." Viking responded. "And from what I hear from outsiders, continuously at that."

Cage glared. "Fuck we care about outsiders?"

"I was just–."

"Let me stop you again, don't speak to my people in that way. If there is a problem with anything, I'll let them know. Not the other way around."

Langley and Helena grinned.

Cage saw no issue in any member of The Stryker Collection speaking up when they desired. Besides, since all of them had access to his mind when he left it open, they knew what he wanted to say anyway.

"I will decide what's necessary to touch on with the Vampire Nation." Cage said. "Me alone."

"The Collective," Viking corrected. "Not the nation."

Helena smiled, loving their frustration.

"Whatever you call it, my answer remains the same. If I need any of you, I trust you'll be here for questions. Until then, back the fuck off."

Cage was done speaking to vampires old enough to have met Jesus. So he left to conduct his meeting.

Standing as tall as the Empire State Building, Cage walked on the stage with The Stryker Collection at his rear. The moment he stood behind the podium he changed his mind and chose to walk in front of it to address his community with his heart.

Besides...many had suffered hundreds of long-drawn-out meetings by The Elders who despite looking as if they were in their late twenties or early thirties, still possessed outdated ways of thinking. The Elders spoke of unity and the importance of sticking together but said nothing of the lawlessness that occurred amongst Collections, which threatened to expose them all. They spoke nothing of a plan needed to provide blood to members who lost their masters due to sun exposure or attack.

To The Collective as a whole Cage was refreshing.

He was the future.

When the cheers settled, he looked upon every one of them. It seemed like forever but his eyes didn't miss a Vamp. He wanted them to know he saw each one of them.

That he felt them.

"I'm often misjudged because I think with the mind of both vampire and Wolf!" He yelled.

A few moaned but chose to hear him out anyway. But the Stryker Collection didn't buckle or fold. They were there for everything their leader said. Besides, he took care of their needs and made sure they were fed.

Heard.

And more than it all, LOVED...

"And although my blood father was Tino, my other father, Magnus, taught me honor. I know what it feels like to crave the sweet blood from Norms whose very existence demand that we take of them...suck of them...and in some cases, fuck them."

More cheers.

"But being raised by a Wolf has afforded me another unique opportunity. I know how they think and I know how, if we aren't careful, they can exploit our weaknesses against us."

"But we aren't weak!" One Vamp yelled from Brooklyn, New York. The Brooklyn niggas, just like the Baltimore and Washington D.C., Vamps, didn't believe in weakness. Their minds couldn't even fathom the possibility. "We are stronger than they think we are!"

Knowing how deeply they felt, Cage did not take the outburst as disrespect.

"I hear you, brother!" He looked at him square on. "I truly do. But before you speak, answer me this..."

"I'm listening!"

"Have you stood in a room of Norms whose blood smelled as sweet as a peach and chose to deny yourself? Were you able to walk away without sucking their blood even though you hadn't fed in days?"

Brooklyn Vamp remained silent. Besides, his right-hand man was there and knew he had yet to showcase such restraint.

"CONTROL YOUR URGES AND CONTROL YOUR FLESH!" He said, reminding them of their motto.

They nodded with understanding.

"Yes, we have weaknesses!" Cage continued. "All species have weaknesses. There's nothing to be ashamed of! And due to the Subterfuge parties, we are being lured to environments that contain the sweetest blood, only to be assaulted by Wolves. And depending on what's used...killed."

And then he grew silent.

And so the room did too.

"But when we know what our weaknesses are, and we can think three steps ahead, we not only prepare and resist their attacks, but we also lay the groundwork for the protection of our species as a whole."

More cheers.

The Elders nodded, now seeing how Cage's charismatic swag was paying off.

The men respected the alpha in his walk. While the women wanted to touch him...to consume him.

"But they have weaknesses too, Ock!" A sexy Philly Vamp yelled. His beard was effortlessly cut and sheened to perfection.

"Indeed." Cage said. "But that weakness is us. And it is this weakness that we must discuss."

By T. STYLES

Uneasy movement and chatter filled the place as the reason for the congregation became clear.

"I don't know why they're attacking us all of a sudden." He lied. "But we have to defend ourselves."

"Is it true that they're eating us?" One Vamp yelled. "Because I heard your ex-wife, Angelina, is responsible."

Cage looked down and back at the Vamp. "All rumors." He lied. "More than anything, they're ripping us to shreds."

"But why?"

"For now I don't know." He hated lying to them, but he felt he had no other choice. Telling them that it was true that Wolves were eating them would lead to battles in the street daily. "So we must dodge traps."

"But how?" A Vamp yelled.

"Control your fucking Collections! Teach them to be smarter. Make sure they are fed and avoid Subterfuge parties. But more than anything, make sure they are taught to be aware of their surroundings. That's it for now."

The moment the speech was over, and Cage walked toward the back with his Collection behind him, they were met with hate from The Elders.

"Why didn't you mention The Fringale!" Viking yelled; his body so close to Cage's they looked like lovers.

"Why would I mention it now?" He stepped back out of respect, but that would be the last step he'd make before shit got violent. "We aren't about to battle the Wolves tomorrow. I need to gain their trust before–"

The blow Cage took to the face by Viking rocked his body.

He was a vampire, so like the Wolves he healed quickly. But that didn't stop the pain.

Upon seeing the blow, the Stryker Collection went the fuck off. They grabbed the nearest Elder to fight back, but because The Elders had lived many years, that made them stronger and more deadly.

The Stryker Collection was no match for their old ass strength.

In the end The Elders beat the brakes off them, leaving them winded and on the floor.

It wasn't even close.

In that moment, The Elders let it be known who was superior. At least physically. "Let me make myself clear." Viking boasted, while The Elders stood over Cage and other members of his Collection. "You aren't in charge. We are!"

By T. STYLES

"Exactly," Marco yelled.

Cage, already incensed, was sure to remember each feature of his face. He would pay for the disrespect. He was certain.

"So when we tell you to do something, it's not a request. It must be done!" Viking continued. "This is your final warning."

As they walked out, Cage glared.

While Viking, Marco, and The Elders smiled.

CHAPTER TWELVE
CHEDDAR

Cheddar had a long day or in Vampire terms a long night.

After helping Onion finalize the designs for his new home, Cheddar needed to get up with his girlfriend Happy. Every other day he was hearing a story about Onion and his Collection which meant he had to clean up the mess. They were sloppy and as a result, made themselves vulnerable to attacks and eventually hate from The Collective as a whole.

So his girl, Happy, gave him relief.

After a long night of love making and blood drinking, he left her house. The moment he closed her door, he could sense he wasn't alone. He hated to be caught slipping, especially tonight since the plan was to lockdown before sunlight.

"You might as well show yourself." Cheddar spoke.

Slowly, Langley came from behind the bush and stood before him. Hands clasped behind his back. "We need to speak."

"How did you know I was here?"

"I'm a member of the Stryker Collection. We are advanced."

Cheddar nodded and wished he could say the same for Onion's folk. "What do you want?"

"I would prefer to do it somewhere else." He nodded toward the street. "I know an approved bar where they serve sweet blood if you can spare the time."

"I'll bite. Let's go."

Fifteen minutes later they were in a bar exclusive for vampires. After taking a few shots of delicious blood Langley positioned his chair to look at him. Cheddar did the same. "My master wants to meet with you."

"I figured as much."

"Will you meet with him? To discuss his business?"

"Just as you stepped outside of your boundaries to violate my privacy and show up at my girlfriend's house, Cage could have done the same. And yet he chose not to."

"You and I both know that master's don't have to be involved with the night-to-night errands. I'm sure the same thing can be said about your master. Onion."

He glared. "He's not my master."

He frowned. "So you tolerate him for free?"

Cheddar moved uneasily. There was history and a reason why he chose to serve Onion. And he certainly didn't feel like explaining it to a man he didn't know. A man who was serving his enemy.

"What does he want? I'm already risking everything by meeting with you."

Langley leaned back "So why did you?"

"Curiosity."

He nodded. "So won't that curiosity be satisfied if you meet directly with my master? What's a few more hours to get your questions answered?"

"Not necessarily true."

Langley leaned forward. "Listen, he doesn't mean you any harm. He only wants to ask a question. And he wants to hear it from you directly. Onion too, if you think he'll come."

"You know what that question is?"

"Does it matter?"

"Ask me." Cheddar pressed.

"Like I said before my master would prefer if you–"

"We're at a Crossroads, young Vamp. I can say no and then you'll get no information at all. Or you can ask me the question that he'll ask and then come across as the hero if you get your answer. With one version you come out as a failure. The other you come out a winner. Which one will you choose?"

He took a deep breath. Langley was in love and perhaps getting this information would convince Cage that he could protect him and love his woman at the same time. So maybe there was something good to come out of all this.

"He met with The Elders one night."

Cheddar smiled. "He's the king. He meets with them all the time. I also heard they fucked Cage and the rest of your Collection up at the Lyric."

"I won't speak on that now. But that incident won't be forgotten. But this particular night I'm speaking about they mentioned something that made him uneasy." Langley continued. "They indicated that you and Onion had a meeting with someone named Anderson which gave you sensitive information. He wants to know what that information is."

Cheddar sighed deeply. "I knew it would come sooner or later."

"Will you tell me?"

"Yes."

"So you will come?" He asked excitedly.

"Easy. I won't enter a trap." Cheddar laughed. "But although I'm not a fan, I respect him as the leader of The Collective. After all, I dedicated my life to Tino before

Onion was put on his side. That means to most vampires, me included, Cage is the true heir."

"I'm waiting on an answer."

"I'll give him the information he wants to know but he has to give me something in return. And this thing is not up for negotiation."

CHAPTER THIRTEEN
CAGE

Helena was beautiful but her body had become a bore.

Cage knew the real reason.

She was so set on pleasing him that she became one dimensional in the bedroom. Something like a robot but a bit more sensuous. So as she sat on top of him, riding him with palms planted in his muscular chest he said, "Get up. Get...just get up."

She didn't hear him at first. She was too possessed by the moment and his thickness that pushed into her body. "Mmmmmm." She moaned.

"Move, Helena." He said more forcefully.

She heard him now. And in shame, she rose up and sat on the bed next to him. "Are you displeased?" She looked down at him.

He had one hand behind his head and the other on his belly. "I don't know."

"Cage...what's wrong?"

He got up and walked to the mini fridge. Grabbing a shot of blood he said, "Yes. I'm very displeased. But it's not your fault."

She placed a hand over her chest. "How? Why are you unhappy?"

He walked over to the window and looked out into the night sky. "I don't know. Something is going on with me mentally. I wish I could make it all make sense. But I can't."

She glared.

With his back turned he could feel her hate. "I feel your rage towards me." He faced her.

"It's because I know the reason you're pulling away."

He walked closer. "If you know what it is, tell me. Maybe you can help us both out."

"Why? So you could leave me?"

Silence.

She took a deep breath. "You still long for her. You've always longed for her. Why are you so attached? Look at everything she's doing to the Collective. She's messy. Whorish. And dangerous."

"Who is her?"

"Don't play games, Cage! I know what this is fucking about! You dismissed her because of her disloyalty. And yet you're giving attention to her now when you should be tasting me."

"Cut it out."

By T. STYLES

"I'm waiting and ready to please you in any way you choose. Body and all. But you hate me for it."

"You sound foolish!"

"Well, prove me wrong!" She made a space on the mattress by tossing the blankets to the side. "Come back to our bed. Lay next to me. Finish what you started."

Suddenly there was a knock at the door. He waited and when he read Langley's mind he said, "I have to go."

"Of course you do." She crossed her arms over her body and threw her weight backwards on the bed.

Cage exited the room and rushed down the hallway. Langley followed him to the lounge. When the door was closed he said, "I see you and Candy are still seeing each other."

Langley cleared his throat. "It's no more than I do any other member of our family."

"I don't see you meeting Jillian that way. Or Bo."

Langley looked down. "I...I love her."

"You're my right hand. I need you focused. So no relationship amongst the family."

He nodded. "I understand, master. It's irresponsible on my part."

Cage sat down. "So will he meet with me?"

"No. But he did have a response."

Cage nodded. "What?"

"He says he does know something. About what you overheard from The Elders."

Cage shrugged. "We knew that already. Did he tell you *what* he knows?"

"No. He has an unusual request, master. One I don't think you will agree to, but I told him I would ask anyway."

"Well what is it?"

"He says that Onion and members of his Collection are growing thirstier."

"So let them eat." He shrugged. "What does that have to do with me in my request?"

"Apparently Onion isn't as organized as you are. You provide for us. Find the best places willing to share their blood. I can't remember a time I had to drink from the source. But he said Onion's too consumed with other matters. Leaving his Collection to their own vices. And so Cheddar, and Onion I believe, wants a place where his vampires are free to drink from the source. He wants Baltimore."

"Again, why's he asking me?"

"Because you are the new king." He paused. "And...since The Elders are trying to do things in the background to prevent a war in the open, maybe he realizes he has to come to you."

Cage knew this was true but he hadn't been forced to make any decision for any specific Collection until that moment. Allowing a Collection to roam freely without penalty was not something to be taken lightly. It meant trouble with The Elders and had to be considered fully.

"Nah...something else is going on." Cage said. "These are outlaws. They have zero respect for our rules. They could just take from sources in Baltimore. They wouldn't need my permission to do something that on his surface isn't illegal anyway. What does Cheddar *really* want?"

He took a deep breath. "There is something else. They need protection from Angelina and her Linas. Everyone is afraid of the Wolves she rolls with. So I wouldn't be surprised if more Collections ask for help in the future."

"I know what I have to do first."

CHAPTER FOURTEEN
ONION

The night sky was noisy as fuck. After all, this was an important reunion that was occurring in the park.

Onion was standing in front of Tino's old house when Cage finally walked up. Although he didn't see the O2 Collection, he smelled them nearby.

He didn't care.

The Stryker Collection also stood hidden in the distance.

Waiting.

"Cage." Onion grinned, walking up to him. "Long time no see. When Cheddar told me about this meeting I almost didn't believe him."

"When I asked to speak I meant over the phone."

"If we did we wouldn't get to see each other." He smiled slyly. "Or have you forgotten we were once good friends?"

Silence.

"I let the past go." Onion continued. "You really should too."

"I don't even know why I'm here. And yet for some reason I was drawn to have this meeting with you. Almost as if I couldn't help myself."

"Are you being romantic?"

Cage glared.

"You've definitely lost your sense of humor. But I'll deal with it. Besides, I need specific things from you."

"I asked to see you due to your request."

"I'm listening." Onion placed his hands behind his back.

"Baltimore?" Cage said. "So now I have to manage your people and my own? It was you who told me about all of the members that you converted. Almost as if to say the little fifty or so that I had wasn't enough."

"I did."

"And yet you come to me for protection."

"And yet you come to me for answers." Onion replied seriously. "Remember? This all started because you wanted something from me and Cheddar. You want to know what Anderson said."

It was true.

The two friends looked at one another for what felt like forever. Cage decided to break the silence. "Why Baltimore?"

"Are you seriously asking?"

"I am."

"People there are the sweetest. And it's close to us. I mean at one point when they ran the campaign "Believe" they seemed to be on their shit but lately it's a city filled with despair. A city filled with blood so succulent we need not go anywhere else. That's why Baltimore."

"I have hope that the city will come around. I believe in–"

"But hope doesn't get us fed, Cage. Does it?" He dropped his fangs.

"There's something about their blood that's very appealing." Cage admitted. "It's probably one of the reasons Angelina can't help but feast there. Are you still in contact with her?"

Silence.

"Onion, do you still talk to Angelina?"

"So that's the real reason you agreed to see me in person?"

"I'm just asking."

Onion sighed. "I did at first. She came over but…she brought Wolves to my house."

"To kill you?" Cage pressed.

"It looked that way but I don't think so. It was a full moon. Her women would've been killed had they

By T. STYLES

tried." He took a deep breath. "Anyway, having a Collection won't help alone anymore. We need to unite. And then at the same time we need to feed. So if we band together and help one another...and look out for each other against her pack and the Linas I think we'll have a chance."

"Why should I trust you, Onion? You've done nothing but cause me grief. Came in between me and my wife and–"

"You and your wife? Have you forgotten that I had her first? And that you stole her from up under me."

"Look who's going into the past now."

"I have loved that woman all my life, Cage. You loved her for one moment and when she didn't meet your standards you abandoned her. So don't talk to me about taking your wife when you and I both know she was always mine. She's still mine now."

Cage was heated, but he couldn't let him see.

"I have agreed to give you Baltimore. But there will be rules. For instance, no drinking until death. No drinking from the source. Use the drug we developed that makes Norms pass out and forget. And then pool blood with needles to feed your people."

"And you call yourself a vampire," Onion joked.

"I'm fucking serious! We aren't killing anyone." He pointed at him. "But giving you protection is something totally different."

"Then it won't help me. I need protection."

"You have over one hundred men, Onion. Can't they look out for–."

"We need the Strykers! I hate to admit it but the way you've taught your Collection, how they see things in advance, makes things different. Makes them superior."

"Why convert all of them niggas if–."

"I didn't want to! I wanted to move alone. Now I got all these mothafuckas that are worse than newborn babies. And now they're being slaughtered in public. Embarrassing the fuck outta me and shit."

He thought seriously. Even though they were not friends anymore, technically Cage was still his king. "I'm not saying no right now. I have to think hard. In the meantime, what's the information you have for me? What did Anderson tell you?"

"Not until I get a firm commitment. Your word that you will help in the event shit hits the fan with Angelina and her crew."

"Have you tried to talk to her since…she tried to kill you?" Cage continued.

"No."

"I could be wrong but maybe we should start there."

"If you think she'll talk I'm with it. But if you ask me, she's still a woman scorned by you."

The night sky was pitch black...

Some stars but not many filtered the scene...

No worries though...tall lamp posts dressed the tree lined street. Due to a recent snowstorm, the pavement was wet and shined like black diamonds. The lights that streamed downward gave a spotlight effect that lit up the block and glowed upon Cage and Onion who stepped into its radiance.

Cage Stryker, fine as aged wine tucked his hands into his black Prada raincoat while Onion, his frenemy, repositioned the collar of his chocolate fur coat for warmth.

From their locations, they looked around.

Searching.

They saw nothing.

"This is a fucking joke," Cage said under his breath.

"You the one that said it needed to be done." Onion looked from where he stood, around the block, peering intensely.

But Cage was so enraged his face crawled into a scowl. "She's unreliable...you can't trust her and-."

"You're still in love." Onion glared. "That's your first and last problem." He pointed his way.

Cage tried to put the anger back in the bag. But it was no use. Onion saw he was still moved by a woman he claimed to hate. "I don't know what you-."

"This is not about you," Onion said, stepping in front of him. "This is about-."

"Get out of my fucking face, nigga."

"Or what?" Onion said.

"Do you really wanna go there with me?" Cage stepped closer. Once friends, the two powerful vampires were sure to rip each other's throats out if things didn't simmer and soon.

"You need to give up any hope you have of being with her." Onion continued. "That's all I'm saying."

"And like *I* said, I'm not interested in anything but business. But even if I was there's not a fucking-."

"With time she won't remember you."

He shook his head and shrugged. "What does that mean? That she won't remember me?"

Silence.

"Onion, what does that–."

Suddenly a woman sang in the distance. They both paused, each looking around to find out where the sound originated from. The beautiful melody grew louder and higher as it continued.

And then it stopped suddenly.

Cage took a deep breath, closed his eyes, and focused on the air around him. His powers had been perfected in a way that made him, well, different. Unlike most vampires, he, and the Stryker Collection, those who took his Fluid in a ceremony, were far more advanced in their capabilities. Mainly because it was important for him that they always be practicing and perfecting so they did. It was known that most vampires had skills available to them that they had not honed.

Focusing harder on the air around him, slowly Cage's lids widened, and he looked upward.

There Angelina was, sitting on a lamp post, her feet dangling as if she were on a merry go round.

When he looked at other lamp posts, he saw the same. Various members of the Linas, her vampire Collection, who were just as beautiful as they were dangerous, all watching him.

"How did you get up there?" Onion asked, somewhat impressed.

She laughed. "Is that what you really want to know? After all, it's been years since the three of us have been *together.*"

"Are you going to come down or not?" Cage said seriously.

"There he goes with that tone." Angelina said sarcastically. "I get the impression that he still believes he owns me."

"I never tried to own you."

"Good, because nobody owns my queen," a member of the Linas said with authority.

"And if you were smart you would remember I am your king." Cage educated.

"We don't recognize you." Another Lina responded.

Tiring of the games, Cage positioned his legs to jump just as high, when suddenly growling from the shadows stopped his motions.

He couldn't see them but he felt their presence.

"Ah, ah, ahn," Angelina said, wagging her finger. "I wouldn't do that if I were you."

Cage inhaled the air deeply. "Wolves."

The hidden growls were replaced with soft feminine laughter upon hearing his words.

By T. STYLES

"So it's true. You are still choosing to keep time with outsiders." Onion yelled. "Fuck is wrong with you?"

She glared. "Where do I start? If I must–"

"If you came here to play games, why even accept the meeting?" Cage interrupted. "It's childish. Even for you."

"Because you're going to die tonight."

Mink, a member of the Wolves, stepped from the darkness.

"So you better have a good enough reason to change my fucking mind." Angelina laughed.

"Can we speak alone?" Cage asked.

"She doesn't want to speak to–."

"I'm talking to her," Cage said, cutting Carmen off.

"I'll allow it." Angelina jumped down and they walked a few feet away, standing next to a box van. Onion, Carmen, Mink, and everyone else were heated.

"I'm begging you to stop. You don't want The Elders as enemies."

She laughed. I don't care about none of that shit. I'm not into politics."

He stepped closer.

"Cage, be careful!" Helena pleaded from a distance. "I got a bad feeling."

He looked at her and glared before focusing back on Angelina who was obviously hurt by seeing her at his side.

"You finally got what you wanted, bitch and you still mad." Angelina taunted Helena.

Helena was about to run but Cage warned her with his eyes. She remained where she was. "Hold your position. I won't say it again."

"You made her your girl, didn't you?"

"Ange-."

"You hurt me."

"Now or then?"

"Both. She was the one person I didn't want you with and you proved my point. That every fear I had with her showing up was valid."

Cage was ashamed. "Listen, I'm here about-."

"If you didn't have your people with you, I would feed you to Mink and watch life slip away from your eyes." She paused. "Stay away from me. This is your final warning." She walked away.

Cage stood at the top of one of his clubs overlooking the vampires who were having a good time.

Strobe lights shone everywhere, and fresh cool blood flowed from the tap. It was the one club he allowed his Collection to go to, when he was present because he owned the bitch and it was secured from Wolves.

As rap music pumped from the speakers, he noticed that two people in particular were enjoying each other far too much. After he already forbade their union.

Despite the music being faster, Langley and Candy danced with one another while looking into each other's eyes. Shane and Ellis stood next to him and looked down also.

"You gonna let them be together?" Shane asked.

"No. It's too dangerous."

"Let love prevail, nigga." Ellis said. "Just 'cause your shit trash right now doesn't mean his has to be."

"It's not that I don't want him happy. It's just that…relationships are liabilities. When you single, nothing can be held against you. But once you choose to be together, there are risks." He looked at them and back at Shane and Ellis. Everyone knew he was talking about Angelina. "When are y'all leaving out?"

"We going tonight." Shane said. "To meet with the leaders of the largest Collections. They hit us back."

"But are you sure you gonna be fine?" Ellis said. "Because we don't like being away from you on these out of state voyages. With Angelina tripping and shit."

"I'm good."

Ellis suddenly leaned over. "Shane doesn't want you to know, but he wants to be converted."

Cage looked at him closely. "Are you...are you serious?"

"Yeah," he smiled. "Says he lives to make sure you are good so he wants The Fluid."

Cage tried to hide the joy in his heart. "I'll talk about —."

"Do it after this Fringale shit. And keep it between us."

Cage nodded. "No doubt. I'll–"

Suddenly every vampire in the club focused on the door. Standing at the entrance was not only a Norm, but also Dickens. The activist from Daylight.

"This nigga bold as fuck!" Shane said. "How did he even find us?"

"Want me to handle it?" Ellis asked.

"I got it." Cage announced.

Cage jumped from the top of the club to where he was and ushered him quickly toward the door.

"Master, what are you doing?" Langley asked. "He's a Daylight! You'll–."

"I have it! Now stay where you are." He shoved Dickens outside. Looking at the entrance of his club, he saw many vampires staring their way. "Go back inside! Now!"

They obeyed.

Although they did it slowly.

"What is this place?" Dickens asked, looking at the building.

"Listen to me, get out of here." Cage said. "Now."

"You're one of them, aren't you?" He paused. He looked him up and down. "Although I can tell…that for some reason you are…different."

"Do you hear me?" Cage persisted. "Get the fuck out of here!"

"I'm on to you. I'm on to all of you."

"If you knew how much your life is in danger, you would've never come here. My advice is not to not only stop what you're doing on social media but to go into hiding too. Now."

"You do know who I am." He grinned.

"Leave."

He looked at the club, at him once again and walked away.

Shane and Ellis came outside.

"That's the lil nigga that be causing strife ain't it?" Ellis asked. "Want me to kill him?"

"No…don't hurt him."

"Don't hurt him! Fuck are you saying?" Ellis begged, his hazy cornea darting around.

"He's alone." Shane said. "We could tuck him in the dirt and–."

"Like I said, don't hurt him. Just see to it that he gets home safe."

"Home safe?" Ellis yelled. "Are you serious?"

"Cage, we have him dead to rights! He's the only one talking about vampires in public. Let's get rid of him!"

"I said no! Don't disobey me! Now see to it that he's safe." He looked at both of them and stepped back in the club.

Shane and Ellis followed orders although they reserved the right to kill his ass if shit hit got crazy.

The moment Cage walked back in the club he approached Langley. "I need you to find out where Angelina sleeps. I'm afraid of what she'll do next.

Because as you saw she still hates that I chose Helena so I believe everything she's doing is because of me."

"When I find her do you want me to kill her?"

"No."

Langley looked disappointed. "When do you want me to go?"

"Now!"

CHAPTER FIFTEEN
CAGE

The rain pounded on the Stryker estate as Arabia stood in front of Cage, her eyes never meeting the floor. He was glaring at her as she was seated in the recliner. "So when will your underground estate be finished?"

"You know that's not what I want to talk about." He paused. "Because you're holding back on me I'm forced to make deals with Onion. I don't want to do that. So I need you."

Her gaze lowered. "Cage, I–."

"Look at me!" He demanded.

Slowly her head rose. She adjusted her red framed glasses. Taking a deep breath she said, "I'm sorry, Cage."

"About?" He knew but he wanted to hear the words.

"The Elders. Viking. Marco. All of it. I didn't know they would react so violently after your speech at the Lyric. But you have to understand, the safety of The Collective is very important to them. So if a few have to die for the survival of the many, they don't see a problem."

"Who is Anderson? And what are they hiding from me? Be straight with me now and I'll always remember you for it." He walked up to her. "This moment, right here, can change everything between us. Tell me the truth and I swear to God you'll have my undying loyalty." He dropped on one knee. "But lie to me and when I exact revenge, I will come to you first."

Arabia rose and walked around him.

"Arabia, what's going on?"

"Cage, I–."

"Come here."

Slowly she walked back and plopped on the recliner. He could tell she wanted to let go of something troubling but didn't know what it was. Softly he took her hand into his.

"Talk to me."

"Cage, you will be angry with me." Looking at his face weakened her.

"What is it, Arabia? What don't I know? Make it clear and I promise I will respect it. No matter how bad."

"But…but…"

"What is it?" He found himself desperate, believing she was on the edge of telling him the truth. "Open your mouth and talk to me!"

"If I talk to you…"

TREASON 3   131

"*When* you talk to me."

"If I talk to you, Cage, it means I die. They would hear of it and...and they will hurt me. They will hurt anyone I love."

Cage was enraged. "I will protect you! I promise! Trust me!"

"I can't."

He was angry that he had to speak to Onion and Cheddar about his situation which meant they had to make deals. He was angry that he had to beg Arabia for information she was obviously not trying to depart with. But after witnessing how The Elders handled him and members of his Collection he knew he had no choice.

"I'm getting pissed, Arabia."

"I know."

"Do you really?"

She took a deep breath. It was time to tell all. "The Elders-."

Arabia was just about to give more information when Langley stood on the other side of the closed-door. Cage knew he was there because he could read his mind. It was bad timing.

"Come inside."

Langley entered per his request and Arabia was shocked. Seeing the level of connection Cage had with his Collection was brand new. Most vampires were not as advanced.

"I must go. But I'll talk to you later."

"Then it will be too late."

"I'm sorry." Arabia said before exiting.

Cage sighed deeply and focused on Langley. "What did you find out about Angelina?"

Langley stood in front of him with wide eyes. "It's worse than I imagined. Me and a few other members were able to trail them from behind. And not only do the Linas and the Wolves roll together, but they may also slumber together too. In the same area."

"So you found her location?"

"Just a general area. The Linas were all dressed like Angelina. And when I tried to get closer, they spread out."

"So the Wolves really are a part of her crew?" He was remembering Bloom and couldn't see how this risk was safe.

Langley stepped closer. "I think they protect her. They guard her. And at the risk of sounding irresponsible I believe they worship her too."

Cage walked away. "How did she get this..."

"Powerful?" Langley asked.

Cage wasn't willing to give her that much credit. Besides, he wanted to know something else. "During the time you trailed them, trailed her, did you see her with a child?"

"No." He frowned. "I didn't. I'm sorry."

He nodded. "Okay…just, leave me alone. I'll call you if I need more information."

Langley exited while Cage flopped in his seat. Something would have to be done about the Linas. The only question was what.

Picking up his phone he called the one man he couldn't stand.

"What is it now?" Onion asked.

"Since we tried talking to her and it ended in threats, I have another idea."

"I hope it doesn't involve hurting her?"

"It's something like a trap. But I want to give her one more chance."

By T. STYLES

Angelina was walking down the block in Baltimore, looking for her next prey.

Instead, Cage bopped up from behind and spoke in her ear. "Fucking come with me, now."

Five minutes later they were in the back of a van with bench seats on the left and right. She was sitting directly across from him.

"Fuck are you doing?" Cage asked, forearms against the top of his legs. "Huh?"

"Why don't you leave me alone?"

"Baby, please stop this shit."

"Baby?" The glare on her face turned into sadness. She wasn't expecting him to be so gentle with her and considerate. "I haven't…I haven't heard you call me that since…forever."

He got up and sat next to her. "The Elders are going to hurt you, Angelina. And I don't want that shit. They gonna hurt our child too. Is that what you want?"

"I never told you I had a child. Who have you been talking to?"

"No one. You just answered my question."

She looked down and back at him. "So you're still doing traps?" She looked at his face. "Why couldn't you do better with me? Why couldn't you be a better husband?"

"Because I had too much going on. And you needed so much from me. While you had the entire day, I only had the night, which I had to share with you, my Collection, and The Collective. But it didn't mean I didn't love you."

She shook her head. "It's because of you I will destroy this world."

"I know you're able. I see that shit. It takes a lot to do what you've done. But I'm begging you not to."

"This is all so...so..." She suddenly lost her words.

"Do you still love me? Because if you do, I'm asking you to stop all this shit. Make it easier on me. Make it easier on all of us."

"You're trying to-."

Cage reached over and pressed her lips upon his. Immediately she stood up and straddled him face to face. Kissing him passionately, she could feel him thickening under her body.

"I missed you so fucking much," she moaned. "I miss you so fucking..."

In a hurry to be with him again, she rose quickly, pushed down her jeans and panties, before kicking them across the back of the van.

By T. STYLES

Cage shoved off his jeans and boxers so that they hung at his ankles. Slowly he eased into her, and she felt like home. "Oh my fuckin'...you're so wet." He moaned.

Up and down she moved until his dick was covered in her juices. She was soft and he gripped her ass cheeks as he pushed deeper into her body. "I miss you, girl," he continued. "I fucking miss you."

Inside of her body he banged to the left, right and around. Then he slid it out gently, causing the shaft to stroke her throbbing clit. He wanted this badly, but he didn't want to rush it, not knowing if or when this would happen again.

He didn't stop until they both reached ecstasy and he came into her waiting body. Breathing heavily, they looked at one another. Both of their fangs hung, due to the sensational feeling.

"I want us to make this work, Cage."

"I want it too. But let's go slow."

"So many things are going on now." She said. "So much shit I set in motion because you...you fucked up my mind. Onion too. And then y'all got the nerve to be rolling with one another again. When it was all I wanted."

"He's not my friend."

"So I'm the common enemy that brought you together?"

"No...it's those Wolves. And your Linas." He paused. "Please stop this shit. You can do it, Angelina."

"Cage...I don't know."

He lifted his hand and stroked the back of her hair as he looked into her eyes. "Stop with this shit you doing out here." He pleaded. "Don't go to no clubs. Don't go anywhere with your Wolves. You do this and you'll be safe. You go against it and I can't be responsible for what might happen."

She looked down. "Will you attack me?"

He raised her chin. "No, Angelina. *You* will be safe. As long as I'm king."

"I'm going to trust you again." She nodded. "To prove it, if you want to see your son, meet me here tomorrow night."

"It's a boy?" He asked with wide eyes. "Are you..you...for real?"

She smiled. "Cage, don't betray me again."

"I won't. I won't. I swear."

The thing was she made other promises.

To Carmen and Mink.

And he did too.

CHAPTER SIXTEEN
THE LINAS

The room was mostly dark, with the exception of neon sprayed black walls that flowed under the black lights. No matter where your eyes landed, everyone looked amazing, even the Norms who with their imperfections sparkled in glowing colors of hot pink, yellow, blue, and the like due to their outfits.

The lavish Subterfuge party was filled to capacity.

Hosted by Onion, it would prove to be a night no one would ever forget.

As vampires roamed around, introducing themselves to unsuspecting Norms, Angelina and the Linas made their way inside. They had heard from a Norm who talked too much on social media, about the event. And since vampire code words like *Subterfuge* and *chambers* were used, she knew that this was an event hosted by blood suckers.

When Angelina walked inside, she and her Linas couldn't believe their eyes. Their mouths watered upon seeing the Norms move about the club.

The Norms, on the other hand, breathed in the vampiric bodies, both male and female, which were all doused with the most amazing perfume and cologne. Their words were feathered with compliments and greetings which made the Norms feel both seen and heard.

And since vampires were insanely attractive, they didn't stand a chance.

"I think we should leave," Angelina said, remembering the promise she made to Cage. "This...this feels a little too perfect."

"I agree," Mink said, looking around. "Something feels off."

"Relax," Carmen said to Mink. The sweet smell floating about made her mouth water and pussy moisten. "We haven't feasted in a while. We good."

"I hope you're right," Mink said. "Because...I...I'm not sure."

"After tonight, we may have to find another way to get revenge on Cage and Onion," Angelina said. "I'll explain when we get home."

"What do you mean?" Carmen frowned.

"I said we'll talk later."

Still not making a move, Angelina looked for a Norm who she believed would bring her sweet joy. There were so many to choose from. And so she said, "I think I see what I want." She paused. "Pick what works for you and meet me here later."

Mink grabbed her hand. "I'm going to remain by the door with my girls."

"Why?" Angelina frowned.

"So I can protect you. Because something feels wrong."

"But aren't they hungry?"

"It doesn't matter." Mink continued. "I have to go with my instincts."

Angelina shrugged. "It's your choice."

"Come here, ladies!" Mink yelled.

Mink talked to her squad and they huddled by the doorway. The beautiful Wolves were disappointed they wouldn't be able to have fun but understood.

Slowly Angelina and her Linas circled the premises, each plotting on what would make them enjoy what was shaping up to be an amazing night. Although Angelina was eager to drink, she had a lot on her mind.

For some reason, in addition to Cage, she also found herself thinking a lot about Onion. The time they spent together as children. How they scrimmaged for food and how at different points in her life, she had to sell her body for them to survive.

While thoughts of him increased, something strange happened that morning.

When she woke up, she noticed she lost a few memories of Cage. Like when she first met him and how long they had been married. Her heart still longed for him, but why was this happening?

She was losing precious thoughts until she looked at her child, who resembled Cage perfectly.

Godric Stryker, Angelina, and Cage's son was a beautiful young man. Despite being a few years old, since he was born to parents who were both full blooded vampires, he grew faster. As of the moment, he had the body of a twelve-year-old. Within a few more months he would resemble a twenty-year-old man, where he would settle a while before eventually resembling early to late thirties. He would remain looking this age for eternity or his death.

When Angelina found what she liked in the club, a handsome man with light skin and low-cut hair, she walked over to him. His body produced the most edible batch of cookie smell she ever imagined.

"Hello there." She winked.

He grinned. "Whoa…this is a first."

"Why you say that?"

"Didn't expect anything as fine as you to walk up on me."

"You're underestimating yourself." She paused. "Come with–."

The first yell came from one of Mink's closest Wolves. When she turned around to see what caused her so much pain, she saw four vampires tearing at her arms and legs until she was a pile of rubble.

When she looked around, more of Mink's Wolves were being attacked.

This was an ambush!

"Fight!" Mink yelled, advising her collection in the Wolves to defend themselves.

It was of no use.

The entire party was a trap.

Onion had successfully planned the set up where there were no less than four Vamps to one Wolf at a time. While Norms were shoved toward the back and out of the way. Due to the care put into protecting humans, Angelina knew this was also Cage's design.

The biggest tell was that she was left unharmed.

The attacks on the Wolves were brutal. And rightfully so because without extreme injury, their wounds could heal.

Mink's Wolves weren't the only ones being slaughtered. She noticed that her vampires were under attack too. Instead of physical injuries, they were injected with doses of Vitamin D. An Elixir that would kill them in very painful ways.

Angelina froze upon hearing her Linas scream in pain.

She hadn't prepared for this.

She failed them.

And then she saw the two responsible.

Both Onion and Cage, standing toward the back, unaware that she spotted them. Despite the destruction and chaos going on around her, they remained still.

Of course the massacre was partially her fault. In an effort to satisfy her Linas and the Minks one last time, she took to targeting her own people. Specifically, vampires in Onion's Collection.

But it didn't stop her from being hurt that they banned together to get at her.

When they were sure the trap worked, they both grinned and went separate ways in the club.

She decided to follow Cage.

Running as fast as she could, she tried to get him. But each time she was blocked, making it hard. Besides, a few members of Cage's Collection kept an eye on their

144

master, which meant they kept an eye on her too. But when some of Mink's Wolves got loose and the Stryker Collection went after them, they momentarily left him undefended.

And there he was, standing by the back door waiting to get out.

With him in her sights, her plan was to grab him from behind and fight him with all her might. She didn't know if she would prevail, but she would try. After all, he was the older vampire.

She took one step closer.

But instead of attacking him, she stopped.

She wasn't sure why but for some reason she couldn't hurt him. Despite what was happening to her own people, in that moment of seeing him she still loved him.

And so she allowed him to walk out the back door.

While Mink stood quietly behind her, watching the entire thing go down.

Cage was with his Collection in a beautiful lake house in Deep Creek Maryland…

It was a celebration!

Cage had facilitated an attack on Angelina's Linas, and the Vampire Collective as a whole was impressed. It showed he could protect them and more than it all, it showed he could lead an army. And it showed that he could target the true love of his life.

The moon was high, and they were enjoying their lives, even though Helena had bouts of a silent treatment she tried to give Cage. But he didn't care. If she wanted to spend every moment thinking about what he might be doing to Angelina, that was on her.

Cage had other objectives. He hosted the party to spend more time with his Collection and to give good news that he was sure would put a smile on everyone's faces. And so, as they swam in the indoor pool, listening to music, Cage rose. "Listen up everybody."

It took a moment but before long, everyone quieted down.

"Langley and Candy, come up here next to me."

When Langley heard his name, he dragged a hand down his face to pull the water away, before helping Candy out. They both seemed uneasy as they stood on opposite sides of their master.

Langley, believing he knew about his continued relationship with Candy whispered, "Boss, I'm sorry I didn't stop seeing her. It's just that–."

Cage put a heavy hand on his shoulder, silencing him instantly. "I want to make the announcement that we have love in the air!" Cage said loudly. "And even though I believe it goes against what I think we should be about as a Collection; I want you to know I understand."

Langley and Candy looked happily at one another.

"Master, what…what are you saying?"

"I want you both to know that I sanction this relationship."

Langley grinned. "For…for real?"

"Get over here, man," Cage said, hugging him with one arm. "But you better be good to her." He pointed in his face.

"You know I will!"

"And you better take care of him," he said to Candy.

"I will."

"Now go enjoy the party."

They hugged each other excitedly.

Cage was about to get back in the pool when suddenly he smelled someone he had known most of his life in the air. It produced chills down his spine, considering how things went down at the Subterfuge party trap.

Exiting the pool, he walked out the back door and looked around. His Collection was so excited about Langley and Candy's union that they didn't notice he was gone. In a since, everyone had let their guards down.

"Where are you?" He asked peering around the woods from where he stood. "I can smell you."

Angelina stepped into view, and it was obvious that she had been crying.

"What you doing here?" He stepped closer.

"You set my Linas up even though you knew I could possibly get hurt too. Why?"

Cage sighed. "Onion and I both told everyone to not harm you."

"But you–."

"I tried to warn you, Angelina! I told you not to indulge in any more parties and you went anyway. There had to be repercussions. But I would never have let you be harmed."

"They killed my Linas. They killed my Wolves too. And you will pay for that shit. And it will be swift."

"I won't let you threaten me."

"I'm making you a promise." She ran into the woods, disappearing into the night.

"What about my son? What about my son? Fuck!"

He was on his way back inside when suddenly he heard screaming inside the pool house. Cage was quick but it seemed like forever trying to get back in. Once he did, he felt a huge sense of dread.

Candy, Langley's girlfriend, was sitting at the back of the pool, in writhing pain, after being secretly injected with D by a Lina who snuck into the party while Cage was outside.

She died in Langley's arms.

Now Cage had forty-nine.

When Angelina returned to her cottage, Mink was waiting at the gazebo. "I saw you let him get away." Mink cried. "At the Subterfuge party. It's because of you I've lost so many good women. Why did you do that?"

She sighed. "I don't know what you're talking about."

"I have served you for years! The least I deserve is the truth. No fucking lies!"

"I couldn't hurt him. I don't know why. And it's tearing me apart that he has done this to us. But I promise you this, I will get revenge. Because the only thing he cares about is secrecy. So the secret will come out about us being real. In your name. And in your Minks names too."

"If only I could believe you." She said before storming away.

Angelina wanted to "feel something" as she walked down a dark street looking for prey. After being hurt by Cage along with the guilt of betraying Mink, she was preparing to bite from the source, which always did the job when she felt someone walking behind her.

"How did you get the D?" Cage said calmly.

She turned around, and he was dressed in all black. More than anything he was alone. "That's what you–."

"HOW DID YOU GET IT!" He yelled, dropping fangs.

By T. STYLES

She looked down and back at him. "My thoughts of you are…getting choppy. Still, I recall many things."

"I'm waiting! You may be Vamp, but we both know who's the strongest."

"What about who's the angriest?"

Silence.

"She looked down. Me having D is so simple. I'm aware that you have it off the market. But for half of my existence I had two vampires in my life. Onion and you. Which meant I wasn't going out into the sun."

"I don't understand."

"I had it to keep my levels up. But I kept it to protect myself. One bottle of oil is all I have left. But it's enough. Isn't it?" She ran away.

PRESENT DAY

After hearing the doorbell ring at Violet's house, Pierre went to answer it immediately. Besides, he wanted her to focus on finishing the book and didn't want any more distractions.

Who he saw on the other side caused him to glare. "Fuck are you doing here, nigga? How did you–."

"How did I get here?" He laughed. "You told me about your writer."

"I never–."

"What if I told you that there's somebody writing our journey. In a book. And that person controls the people we meet. The situations that happen to us. Even if we live or die. And that I can get access to that person. Would you believe me?" He said, repeating the exact words he told him a while ago.

Pierre buckled upon hearing the words he uttered to him. "But I thought you assumed I was lying."

"Things were beginning to happen. Things I couldn't explain. But I believe you now."

"It doesn't matter anyway." Pierre glared. "I have the writer right where I–."

"Pierre." Violet said, walking up behind him. "Who is…who is this?"

By T. STYLES

Needing or wanting no introduction, the stranger walked around him and toward Violet. "My name is Kehinde. May I enter?"

She smiled. "Kehinde? Like the artist?"

He nodded. "May I come inside?"

"Of course."

Kehinde stepped inside quickly angering Pierre.

"Wow, I never met anyone with that name before so...so it's refreshing." She couldn't get over the man's striking good looks. She gazed back at Pierre. "Are all of your friends this handsome?"

"He's not a friend."

"Oh...if he's not a friend who is–."

"Your grandmother's editor." Kehinde interjected.

Pierre laughed. He felt he had him right where he wanted now. All he had to do was prove him to be a liar. "Let me get this straight. You expect us to believe that you know her grandmother? And that you worked personally with her."

"I don't expect *you* to believe anything. As you just admitted, I don't even know you. I am here to work personally with Violet. Nothing less nothing–."

"You're a fraud!" Pierre laughed louder.

"Again, since you already mentioned, and I confirm, that you do not know me, how would you know I'm lying?"

Pierre was unraveling. As he stood in front of Kehinde, he jammed his hands under his armpits.

"Are you okay?" She asked Pierre.

He had to get himself together if he wanted to regain control of the situation. "I'm fine, my sweet Violet."

"Oh brother." Kehinde said under his breath, upon hearing how he spoke to Violet. It was obvious that he definitely dug his fingers into her life. But Kehinde had something for that shit.

"But he's right, I am being rude." Pierre placed a hand on Violet's shoulder. "And I'm sorry you saw me react this way."

"Are you sure you're okay?" She asked.

"Yes. Of course."

She smiled and focused on Kehinde. "If it's true that you are my grandmother's editor, what are you doing here?"

"First, Violet, I want to apologize." Kehinde stepped closer. "I know what it feels like to lose someone."

"Her grandmother isn't dead yet, dummy," Pierre snapped.

By T. STYLES

"Dummy?" Violet said. "I never heard you speak like this."

Kehinde grinned.

"I didn't mean to be so drab." Kehinde stepped closer. "Illness of this magnitude often resembles death."

His presence overwhelmed her. Similarly to how she felt when she first met Pierre. What was it about those two men that consumed her?

"It's okay." She sighed. "I'm still hoping she'll pull through."

"I heard it doesn't look good. So-."

"Explain the storyline." Pierre interjected. "If it is true that you are the editor, explain the storyline of the book." He smiled, having been full of himself. "Violet has a right to know if you're able to handle the job or not."

Kehinde walked past them both and toward the bookshelf. "Your grandmother created an epic saga." He picked one of the books up. "Although her stories are about vampires and Wolves, she went so much deeper. These characters were able to portray compassion and humanity."

"Everyone knows it's about vampires and Wolves." Pierre grinned. "We want more details."

"Pierre…please stop." She spoke. "I want to hear from him."

The smile washed off his face.

"The saga is sweeping but it is about two friends who split later in life and became enemies." Kehinde continued. "All over the love of a woman."

Pierre glared.

"And the recent book, to be named Oignon, will finish this saga." Kehinde smiled because he did his homework prior to coming over. "And I will help you do just that. Before it's all said and done, you will have a finale worthy of your sweet Abuela."

Wow, how did he know she called her Abuela?

Easy. He visited the one man who was always seen with her grandmother before she got ill. How was she to know he went to the lawyer first, and forced the details out of him?

"So…you do know the story." She said, placing a hand over her heart.

"Anybody could–."

"That title wasn't released." Violet said, cutting Pierre off. "He had to have learned it from her." Needing the help, she rushed up to him, wrapped her hands around him and exhaled. "I'm so glad you're here!"

By T. STYLES

Kehinde smiled and mouthed the words, "Hey, Onion."

CHAPTER SEVENTEEN
ONION

As Onion sat in his car in the same location he always did when he waited for Angelina, he thought about the Subterfuge party that was a trap for her clan. With Cage's help, they took out over half of her Collection and many of Mink's Wolves. Now she was weakened.

Onion felt the weaker she was, the more liable she would be to return to him.

The event was a major success for them.

And an epic failure for Angelina.

Unlike in the past, this time Onion didn't have to wait for long for Angelina to appear. After ten minutes, a motorcycle came blasting up the street before parking alongside his car. Popping her helmet off, she glared.

"Angelina…" He spoke.

Instead of walking out to him she paced next to her bike. A few seconds later she took a deep breath and said, "I can't believe you tried to kill me with Cage."

He glared. "Wait…are you fucking serious?"

"Yes! Isn't that what you tried to do? By linking up with Cage and his Collection? I can't–."

"First off nobody tried to kill you. We went after your people."

"An attack on my people is an attack on me!"

"You're running with fucking Wolves! Putting us all at risk. To top it all off, you targeted my people first. People in your Collection which you continuously forget since I MADE YOU! What did you expect me to do?!"

"You betrayed me."

"I'm disappointed. Because you're stronger than this, Angelina."

"What does that mean?"

"You started this war! So stop crying over dead soldiers."

"I lost so many...so many good–."

"Wolves. So fuck 'em. All of 'em." He paused. "I didn't want to hurt you like this. I have loved you from the first day I laid eyes on you. I loved you even when you became his fucking wife. And I love you now."

"Too much happened last night, Onion."

"Then we move past it. It's called life."

"Doesn't make it hurt any less." She looked down.

He walked up to her. "I first want to say I'm sorry."

"For what?"

"Everything I did to you in the past. And I know we will never be how we were when we were children. But it doesn't mean we can't forge a new relationship now. One that's built on trust as adults. As vampires."

"I will never trust you again."

"Then you do yourself a disservice."

She looked down and took a deep breath. "I don't even know why I'm here. I hadn't planned on coming. I planned to meet my squad and let them know that we will get through this. And then it was like... like..."

"You heard my voice in your mind?" He grinned sinisterly.

"Yes." She looked at him closer. "What's happening?"

He smiled. "I'm your master."

"You know something else don't you, Onion?"

"Maybe."

"It has something to do with my memory. And me forgetting parts of my life?"

"Angelina..."

"You're involved with this shit! I know it!"

"Explain." He grinned.

"I...I find myself not being able to hold onto memories." She placed her hands on both sides of her head. "Memories of myself and Cage."

By T. STYLES

"You said you wanted to forget your past with him. Why do you care?"

She ignored him as she continued to speak. "It's not until I see the face of his son that everything floods back. And I remember who he is."

He glared. "His child is alive?"

"Of course."

Onion looked down remembering the past. When Cage learned that Onion had converted her, he took one of the members of her Fluid line and killed him with Helena's help. "But he poisoned someone in the line. The baby should not have survived."

"He did survive. And he is well. And protected."

He looked off. "That means by now he should be around thirteen or twenty something years –."

"Why are you asking questions about my son?"

"Where is he?"

"I have to go. I just came here to say, wait until you see what I do next."

She got on her motorcycle and roared away.

It was total chaos on movie night.

And they were only thirty deep. Fifteen Linas, including Angelina. And fifteen Wolves.

Angelina stood in the back while her Linas ripped through the theater, biting people on the neck as they watched a blockbuster movie.

Screams.

And pleas to understand what was happening rang out.

When people tried to leave, the Minks, helmed by Mink herself, pushed them back inside. A young girl with an aisle seat, was wide eyed and trembling. The screen she was once watching, was now covered by shadows of people running about the theater.

And then Angelina approached.

She was beautiful and yet vicious which brought on a sudden panic attack. Standing over top of her at first, Angelina reduced her height and said, "No one will harm you."

Screams continued to ring out.

The girl nodded.

"Are you on social media?" Angelina asked.

The girl nodded again.

"Give me your phone."

She fumbled through her purse and located her cell. Angelina took it, rose, and recorded the melee. Using the flashlight, she was careful to zero in on necks being bitten by beautiful women with blood-soaked fangs.

When she was done, she uploaded the video to the girl's social media account and Twitter page.

"I'm going to hold this for a while. Do you have a problem with that?"

"N...no." She shook her head rapidly.

"Good. Now go."

She trembled and then a stream of liquid exited her body, dampened the burgundy seat beneath her and dripped to the floor.

"Leave now before I change my mind!" She dropped her fangs.

Seeing the horror, she caught wheels as she bolted toward the front door. When she was there, Angelina nodded for Mink to let her go and when she disappeared Angelina grinned.

Later that night she went to bars, clubs, private events and more, doing the same thing. She'd choose a woman with the least sweet smell. Grab her phone. Recorded the scene and let her go.

After looking at the videos on the internet and seeing the pain she provoked she smiled.

Cage was resting in the hot tub when Langley entered with a look of horror on his face. Still broken up about losing Candy, he was down these days.

"What is it?"

"Angelina."

He glared. "What about her?"

He walked the phone over to him and Cage shook his head in disdain as he focused on all the media. *How could she be so fucking stupid? How could she be so reckless?* He thought.

"You want me to do anything?"

"I got ideas. That is if The Elders don't get her first." He eased out of the hot tub and snatched a towel off the rack. "Fuck!" He sighed. "But first, I have to address The Collective. You go do your thing."

"I'm on it."

Before he left, Cage said, "I'm sorry about Candy."

He nodded to avoid crying and rushed out the door.

Karen Michaels was running on her treadmill at night looking at the videos on her TV screen on social media of "Apparent Vampire Attacks". She saw the grizzly footage but couldn't believe it was real.

Grabbing her cell phone she called her blogger friend Porsha. "Girl, I was just about to call you. You seeing this?"

"Fuck yeah! I'm trying to see how they did this shit? Like the teeth look like they are literally going into the neck."

"You don't think it's real, do you?"

"It's impossible! This would mean…"

Suddenly there was a knock at her door. "Let me call you back. I'm expecting a date."

"But I heard you on the treadmill. Are you at least going to wash your ass?"

"Nope! He likes it this way." She giggled and ended the call.

When she stopped the treadmill and hopped down, she grabbed her towel and dried her face. Opening the door without looking through the peephole she was shocked to see a beautiful man standing before her. His skin was without flaws and his eyes were piercing.

"I thought you were going to come a little later."

"Nah, Mommy. I wanted to see you now. Are you going to let me in?"

Sure.

"I need you to say the words come inside."

"You so silly." She shook her head. "Come inside."

Once Langley was through the doors he was led to the living room where her treadmill was. Still on the screen were videos of Angelina's attacks. "You don't believe this shit do you?"

"Not really." She said. "Do you?"

"Fuck no. One of the girls in the video is an actress."

"For real?"

"Hell yeah. In several movies. This just an indie project."

She sat next to him. "Why do you think they did this?"

"To get a movie deal." He grabbed her hand and she straddled him. "Isn't it obvious? And if I were you, I would tell the other bloggers you roll with the same thing."

"But I–."

"Tell them the same thing." He said, seducing her with his eyes.

Now in a trance she said, "S...sure. It's...it's all fake."

He grabbed the remote, turned off the TV and fucked her right.

CHAPTER EIGHTEEN
CAGE

The Lyric theater was packed with the top members of The Collective nationwide. After Angelina's rage parties, over the past few months Cage made promises and rules that were respected by many. With a need for normalcy, he created what could only be described as a police department whose primary focus was to provide protection.

And they were great.

Trained by Cage they were called, The Mag. And on God, they brought order.

Older vampires loved the plans while younger vampires fell in line for the moment. Although many reserved the right to cut up if the rules were too restrictive.

With the Stryker Collection standing behind him, Cage approached the podium, facing a packed audience. "I have been receiving your messages about the blogs and Vamp attacks. And I have heard your voices. Just like with all of you, it's important to me that we breed, convert, and quench our thirst."

Loud cheers.

By T. STYLES

Also present, in the back of the room, The Elders were getting annoyed that he had yet to utter the word...Fringale.

"And to show that I understand how important it is that we thrive, I have designated one city and once city only for you to pool and collect your blood. Before I release the name of that city, I understand that it will be too far for some of you to travel regularly. Particularly those of you who live on the west coast. So tonight I will give the list of distributors who will make sure, with a small fee of course, that you get your share of blood. This will provide specific channels for you and your Collection's survival without alerting the Norms that we exist."

More cheers.

"That city is Baltimore."

The room silenced.

"Is Baltimore blood that good?" One vampire yelled.

Cage nodded to a member of his Collection and he was brought a cup to taste. The liquid rolled down his throat and he grabbed his dick with his free hand. "Damn."

Heavy laughter filled the room.

"To ensure that we go undetected, those with only the sweetest smelling blood will be selected from nightclubs that we currently own. More nightclubs are being purchased now to handle the demand. These people will be brought to a location of our choosing. Where their blood will be drained with the use of narcotics to knock Norms out while we collect."

"But...what do we do with the bodies?"

"We will not drain them to completion. I do not condone death. Of any Norm."

More glares.

"But what are they going to say when they wake up weak?"

"Nothing. Instead of teeth marks, there will be faint evidence of a scar on their arm. They'll think that they've suffered a hangover. This will allow us to go undetected."

"It won't work." Someone yelled from the audience.

Cage looked behind himself at Langley. "Run the video."

The lights went down in the theater.

For the first time ever, Cage showed his process for pooling blood for his Collection. A party would begin at a club owned by Cage. Once the music and drinks were poured, selections were made and those people were taken to the back room which was set up for extractions under the influence of a drug. Norms sat in chairs like those dentists used and blood was taken painlessly without them knowing.

When the video was done the lights returned.

"I realize this takes the fun away from drinking from the source. But we must change how we move about the world. And from this point on, since we're under attack by–."

"Your wife!" Someone yelled.

Cage focused on the man. His name was Archie and he ran a Collection in Japan.

"Yes, by my ex-wife."

"I hear she runs with Wolves." Archie continued, standing up. "Some say you allow her to…let Wolves attack your own people."

"Did you also hear that I weakened her numbers? And that I will continue to do so until she's no more?"

"Why are Wolves attacking us all of a sudden?" A Hollywood vampire asked. "What's going on?"

"We're at war and–"

"The war can be stopped!" Viking yelled from the back of the theater as he stood in front of The Elders. "Tell them how, Cage!"

"You aren't an invited speaker here!" Langley advised pointing his way. "Wait your turn or–."

"Or what?" He bucked. "We kick your ass again?"

"Get the fuck up outta here with your old ass!" A southeast DC nigga exclaimed. "Y'all niggas been talking shit for years. This the first time we heard a plan that would allow us ALL to eat."

Viking glared and exited the hall with the other Elders following behind him.

The moment they exited, Tatum, covered by Row, Canelo and Shannon entered. Since they were Wolves and having just heard that they were still attacking vampires, every Vamp in the room rose and dropped their fangs.

Shit was crashing down around Cage for sure.

In defense mode, the Wolves buckled ready to attack until Cage raised his hand. "Stop! This is my brother!"

The vampires relaxed slightly.

"This won't be long!" Tatum yelled. "I come here as a personal reminder, Cage. You have four days to produce Flow and Bloom. Or else!" They walked out the door.

CHAPTER NINETEEN
CAGE

After the speech, The Elders rushed toward Cage's Benz van that was tailed with even more vans belonging to the Stryker Collection. Viking, Marco, Paris and other members posted up and waited for him to come outside.

"He is insolent!" Viking yelled with tight fists clenched. "He doesn't respect history and he doesn't respect us!"

"At first it was what we loved about him," Marco said. "But if we want him to do the job we must be careful. He's getting stronger with The Collective. Which means he's–."

"Still a baby fucking vampire who's less than one hundred years old. Less than fifty even. We have spanned this earth thousands of years and he doesn't get that there is a hierarchy of–."

"Of what?" Cage said with the Stryker Collection walking toward them. "Fuck y'all niggas talking about now?"

Viking stepped to him and almost shivered when his Collection circled them with guns aimed in their direction.

He laughed; despite being shaken. "Your age and immaturity's showing. Surely you know we can't be killed with bullets."

Marco, and the others waited silently.

Viking looked at the guns and back at him. "Didn't you hear me? Why are you still aimed?"

"The bullets are doused in D." Marco said. "I can smell it from here." He was horrified.

Now Cage smiled.

"How are you able to get it? Nothing real exists on the market but synthetic crap and —."

"I own warehouses of this shit. And I keep it for moments like this." Slowly he stepped closer. "I'm tired of you, Viking. So you will have no more access to me."

"You're making a big mistake. You need me! Because in a matter of months we will be eaten alive unless we select a percentage!" Viking yelled. "And yet you don't care. You carry on with these speeches and are delaying the inevitable. Who's going to the battle?!!!"

"If you think I don't care, you know nothing of me."

"It's what I feel!"

Cage took a deep breath. "You know, I had great respect for you at first. All of you. I figured you must know something that I don't since you lived sooo fucking long. And now I realize you don't know shit. So I'm no longer interested in having you near me."

"You are nobody without us." Viking said. "We gave you the throne and we can take it away!"

Cage laughed. "Yeah, aight."

"I made you! We all made you! And what do you do? Give them Baltimore. Allowing an open market which will let them run wild. And I hope you aren't stupid enough to believe they won't drink in their states and countries."

"I expect crime. No more or less than crime committed by Norms. But what it also does is buy time."

"I don't understand–."

"Whether you understand or not is not my problem. But I want you to know this, if I find out you're lying to me about anything I will have you dragged into the sunlight and burned alive."

"Treason! You just threatened an Elder," Marco said. "Is that really what you want to do?"

"Nigga, suck my dick."

Viking's mouth unknowingly opened in horror.

With nothing else to say, Cage eased into his van along with the members of his Collection and drove off. The Elders stared at them until they disappeared from sight.

CHAPTER TWENTY
CHEDDAR

Cheddar and Cage enjoyed blood drinks laced with tabasco sauce in the root cellar of Cheddar's private apartment. He kept the location secret so as to have a place that only he knew about.

And yet he had chosen to trust Cage.

Because he...well...was trustworthy.

"This is delicious," Cage said, sipping the drink slowly. "But it's not from Baltimore, is it?"

Cheddar smiled. "I hope you don't mind. But I imported this before the agreement."

Cage nodded. "You mean the agreement you asked me for? To sanction off Baltimore for blood pooling. I expect there to be a transition period." He laughed. "Besides, this is good."

Cheddar chuckled and grew quieter. "I have been wanting to speak to you since Tino passed. At the risk of seeming disloyal to Onion, you're our rightful king. And I know this."

"And yet you aligned with Onion anyway."

"It's because before your father died he was the man he chose by his side. And I was loyal to Tino. I'm still loyal to Tino now. Which leads me to his direct bloodline."

"He chose Onion because I wouldn't bend."

Cheddar nodded, liking him even more. "Very rarely I say this but I'm going to now. I can see why you're chosen to lead us. To have been raised by Wolves and yet born of vampiric blood makes you versed on both species. But it's your bravery and kindness that makes you worthy of being a king."

"I'm not a king. I'm not kind either."

"You are a king. Let's not play games. You know it's true."

Cage rose. "I…I know what I must do. I just haven't settled into the idea of–."

"You still love her." He interrupted.

Cage took a deep breath. "How do you know I–."

"You let her leave after you set the perfect trap."

Cage looked down.

"And yet if you let her live, she will be the death of The Collective, Wolves and Norms alike. She is powerful. And there is nothing more energizing than a woman who is driven by revenge."

"Why you telling me this?"

"Because you have to understand that you won't be able to tame her. I saw it with my own eyes. She had all intentions of killing a man she's known since she was a child." He sipped. "I was the one who put her out of Onion's house. She was going to let the Wolves get at him." He paused. "You're scared to make a move on her directly because she has your son."

Cage glared.

"Yes," Cheddar grinned. "I know all."

"I need to see him."

"By now he would be somewhere between twenty and twenty-two. And no doubt being inundated with many reasons to hate you. And also, similar to you, being surrounded by Wolves, she could use him as a weapon against you. Against all of us."

Cage was growing annoyed. It was time to skip the subject. "What do you know?" He reclaimed his seat. "About The Elders? And where is Onion?"

"Lately he's been missing." He took a deep breath.

"And yet everything seems to still be working in his favor." Cage responded.

Cheddar smiled.

"What of The Elders?" Cage repeated. "I need you to honor the agreement and tell me now. I gave you Baltimore. The Mags will provide protection in the clubs. I'm tired of waiting for your end of the bargain."

Cheddar nodded. "I'm going to tell you something you won't believe. Something you may find it hard to understand but I want you to hear me out anyway."

"I want to–."

"I mean, I need you to allow me to tell my story uninterrupted." Suddenly Cheddar smiled and looked around the empty cellar. "Your Collection is near."

Cage shrugged. "They've been near all along."

"I can feel their energy now." He nodded. "It must be because you are getting anxious about what I'm going to say. Are you nervous?"

Cage couldn't deny it, especially since he opened his mind allowing them to hear every word.

"You have that power? The power to allow them to hear every word said, don't you?"

Cage remained silent.

"Tino had the same. And if I were you I would shut them out for a moment. Because what I'm about to tell you will change everything."

As Cage braced himself he did as instructed, closing his Collection off mentally. "What do you know?"

"When you and Onion first went to war, someone reached out to me. He chose me because of my relationship with Tino. It was then that I learned of what is to happen to us and the Wolves. The man's name is

By T. STYLES

Anderson. He's a thousand years old but looks early thirties. He claimed that every few hundred years, vampires must be sacrificed."

"I know this already."

"Uninterrupted." Cheddar said. "That was the agreement."

Cage took a deep breath. "Continue."

"Every few hundred years a percentage must sacrifice themselves. And what you don't know is based on the creed, The Elders are supposed to go first. It's part of the unwritten pact to sacrifice a portion of the vampire population to the Wolfpack. Once The Elders are sacrificed, all is calm until the next couple hundred years."

"Wow." He dragged a hand down his face.

"But lately The Elders refuse to make the sacrifice first. Instead of dying on the battlefield, they work to manipulate others through a leader. This cycle, that man is you."

Cage was in so much rage he trembled. "You mean to tell me that these niggas are the percentage?"

"Yes."

"They fucking played me! And I...I knew something was up!" He looked downward. "I knew something was off. Arabia…Viking kept…kept pressing me. Kept trying to push me."

"You can use this anger against them…you can be something greater. For The Collective. And I will follow you."

Cage took a deep breath. "I can't let them get away with this shit."

"I know. So what's the plan?"

"I have to see my brother first. I need the Wolves."

Tatum sat on a chair that resembled a throne in the Wolves headquarters. After hearing Cage's story about his siblings being tucked away, he was angry. Ten Wolves, Row, Shannon and Canelo stood behind him and the Stryker Collection with Cheddar at his side stood behind Cage.

"So you did to our sister and brother what that woman, Savannah, did to us?" Tatum asked slowly. "By locking them away again?"

"I told you why. She was hurting other vampires and even came after me. Flow too. Short of having someone else kill them, I tried to protect them."

"Came after you?" Tatum said. "What does that mean?"

"I believe she and her friend tried to eat me."

Tatum glared and dragged a hand down his face. "This...this shit is fucking me up."

Row stepped up. "This is what I was telling you about. With your father. He ate Vamp flesh before and as a result, couldn't have Cage around once he took The Fluid. What we don't know is why." Row took a deep breath. "Then to find out Bloom and her friend did the same thing to other Vamps." He shook his head. "He was right to lock them away, Tatum. We don't want to start a war due to a few isolated events."

"Is it isolated though?" Tatum asked. "What's going on, Cage? I feel like you know more." Tatum stood up and slowly approached Cage. "Why are Wolves attacking vampires?"

"I don't know." Cage lied. "But what we need is to prevent things from getting out of control."

Tatum didn't believe him. "This is too much but..." he looked back at Row and again at Cage. "I need to know why you're telling me this now."

"I could lie."

"I prefer if you didn't."

"I'm telling you now for two reasons. First, I was lost on what to do with Flow and Bloom. I mean I knew I couldn't let them go without care since Bloom literally-."

"Tried to attack you with her friend in your sleep."

"Yes." Cage didn't want to tell them at this time that the cravings would eventually be on a larger scale. Although at some point he would no longer be able to hide this fact. "At the same time, I need to know that if they're released they'll be looked after. I need to know that they won't be allowed to kill one of us. Or even me."

"You have my word!" Row yelled. "They will be protected."

Tatum looked back at him and glared.

"I mean, we'll take Tatum's lead." Row continued.

Tatum took a deep breath and faced his brother. "You have *our* word. And you have *my* word that I will not let any harm come to you or the vampires. Now what is the second reason you're telling me?"

"I need your help. I got too many sucka ass niggas around me. I need to remedy that shit."

Arabia was in her room making love to a young vampire no more than seventeen-years-old in Norm age, which put him in his thirties. Although he was inexperienced, she applauded his care with her body and so she sexed him as often as she pleased.

And Ermy, appreciating being under her tutelage, enjoyed being there for her every time she called.

From behind he rammed into her body, while pawing at her huge breasts. The red glasses she was wearing were as steamed as her pussy that dripped with enough juice that could be measured in a cup.

When she felt herself cumming, she pushed back so hard, threatening to knock him off the bed. But he maintained the reins of her nipples, until he exploded into her pussy.

When they both were done, she fell face up on the bed and he laid beside her. "You are always so soft...and wet."

She smiled. "Thank you, gentle boy."

He laughed. "Where does your mind go when we make love?"

"On you of course."

"No it doesn't. I'm not intelligent, but I'm smart enough to know that's a lie. You have been uneasy all day."

She sighed as Cage's face flashed through her thoughts. "It's a long story. A very complicated one too."

"We're listening," Cage said standing in the doorway with Helena to his left and Langley and Cheddar to his right.

She jumped up and shielded her body as Ermy kindly exited the bed. Before leaving the room, he stopped by Cage. "I hope I made you proud, king."

"You have." He winked.

Arabia's eyes widened and her breath quickened. They had used her sex partner to set her up.

Cage stepped forward, sitting on the edge of her bed. Reaching over, he removed her glasses and wiped away the condensation that had formed while fucking with the edge of his shirt. Next he replaced them on her face.

"That nigga looks just like me." He laughed. "Good taste."

"So…this is it?" She asked while trembling.

"I warned you to tell me everything you know." His fangs dropped. "And you...you lied to me. Why couldn't you be honest? I gave you a way out. You didn't take it."

"But you can't kill me. Technically you shouldn't be in here without an invite because-."

"You are in a vampire's home. All are welcome."

She sighed. "Cage, please. I'm begging you to not do this. Who will tell you things you don't know about? Who will make sure you are aware of-."

"He'll be fine," Cheddar interrupted. "I got his young ass."

She eyed him. "Tino's right hand." She shook her head in disgust. "He's the same man who took your enemy's side when shit kicked off. And yet you trust him more than me?"

"In this moment, yes." He placed a hand on her cheek. "If only you had been more loyal. Who knows what could have been." He reached over and kissed her lips.

Standing up he looked at Helena and Langley. "Finish her."

Barring knives, they walked in and slit her throat.

Since she was a Day Walker she would be dead in under one minute.

Viking and Marco were in their salon having drinks and speaking of the future.

"I can't believe his insolence!" Viking yelled. It had been days since he saw Cage and still he was pissed. "He doesn't even care that we alone hold his destiny in our hands! Told me to suck his dick and everything. What kind of shit is that?"

"We should have taken him out when we had the chance. But trust me, we will not make that mistake again."

"No we won't. In fact, along with Cage I have placed a hit on his son's head as well as Angelina's. I don't need his son avenging his father's death in the future."

Marco smiled. "A line has been made."

"Exactly."

Suddenly two guards rushed into the room. "I'm so sorry, sir." The youngest of the two said. "They're Day Walkers and...and I couldn't smell them at first. But they are on the property."

By T. STYLES

Vikings eyes widened. "I don't understand what you're talking about."

"I think Day Walkers are here to do you harm!"

"They were able to get on our property? How did they even know where we lived?"

"Sir, I don't know."

"What about the rest of our men? The other guards?"

"They killed one and the others ran. In fear for their lives."

"What are you talking about? How?"

Slowly Shane and Ellis, Cage's most trusted Day Walkers entered.

"Who are you?" Marco yelled.

"And do you know who we are?" Viking said with all the power in the world. "Because we will destroy your whole-."

"Sit the fuck down, man!" Shane and Ellis sat in beautiful chairs across from the men. "We don't mean you any harm." Ellis continued. "Sit."

"We demand that you two get out of here. Or we will-"

"Take a fucking seat!" Ellis yelled louder, pointing at the floor.

When they heard the slow growling of Wolves and saw Tatum, Row, Canelo, and Shannon's huge frames in the doorway, they did as they were told. They also held guns laced with D bullets.

"You got anything in here to drink but blood?" Shane asked.

"What do you think?" Viking responded sarcastically.

Shane and the crew laughed.

"If you don't mean us harm, what do you plan to do?"

"Nothing," Ellis said. "We just want to watch you sleep."

The Wolves took their positions on the floor. When they turned their heads for a moment, Marco took off running by dipping through a secret passageway in the wall.

Shane was about to chase him.

"Let him go!" Ellis said as the Wolves surrounded, Viking. "This one will do." He grinned at him. "Cage called this nigga by name."

At first Viking was confused. But they didn't harm him. At least not at that moment. Instead hour after hour passed and they continued to watch him.

Of course he did his best to remain up but nothing worked. Eventually, he succumbed to the hour and fell into a vampire slumber. The moment he did, Shane and Ellis, with the Wolves at his side, drug him into the sun, watched and recorded as he was burned alive.

CHAPTER TWENTY-ONE
CAGE

Bloom and Flow were eating burgers more raw than cooked when Cage entered the apartment he had them tucked away in. The moment Bloom smelled his scent, her entire body got energized.

Walking inside with Langley at his left and Helena at his right, he turned around and said, "Wait outside."

"But she craves you and–."

"Wait outside!" He said cutting Helena off.

"Yes, *master.*" She said with an attitude.

When they were gone he walked up to his siblings who were both seated on the sofa. "I'm letting you go today."

Bloom placed a hand over her heart while Flow nodded.

"For how long?" Flow asked.

"Permanently."

Bloom cried softly. "I knew you wouldn't let us stay here forever. I knew you would eventually set us free." She walked up to him but he stopped her with a palm to the chest.

"You...you are afraid of me?"

By T. STYLES

"We have to keep our distance from one another. For your own good."

She nodded her head slowly. "I understand."

"There are some prerequisites too."

"Like what?" Flow asked.

"You won't have access to me alone. Ever again."

Bloom's eyes widened. "So not even to see you? To tell you how I'm doing?"

"I can't take the risk right now. Maybe later in life." He paused. "Basically what I'm saying is I trust you. But not your nature. That makes me unsafe."

He walked toward the door and stopped. "I'm sorry that I had to keep you here. And if you want revenge I will understand." He looked at Flow. "But you need to know if you do, I will be waiting. And I will be ready."

He walked outside as Tatum walked inside. The moment Bloom saw his face she rushed up to him and cried in his arms.

Once outside of the underground apartment Helena said, "They will be a problem."

"Stay out of it," Cage warned. "These are family matters."

"We are your family too."

Ignoring her he looked over at Langley. "Any word on Angelina? Any more sightings?"

"No."

"She's too quiet. Something is up."

Twenty minutes later, Cage with Cheddar at his side, was led to a building. Once through the doors, he was taken toward an apartment. Fifteen minutes later they were allowed inside a unit on the lower level.

A man wearing a red beanie stood outside the door on guard. Once realizing it was the vampire king and Cheddar, he allowed them in.

Anderson was seated on a mahogany-colored leather recliner. Over one thousand years old, he looked every bit of thirty-five. His skin was vanilla, and his eyes were like caramel candies.

Anderson smiled. "You're doing well for us."

Cage shrugged. "I'm still trying to understand most of this. Which is why I'm coming to you."

He nodded. "I don't need to tell you what I'm about to say but I will. Your life is in danger."

Cage nodded. "You mean The Elders?"

"Who else?"

By T. STYLES

"I know. And I have a plan to protect me when they come. One that will be controversial." He paused. "But I need to know about The Cravings. How do they work?"

He took a deep breath. "When The Cravings are at an all-time high any Wolf that's in the presence of a vampire will not be able to control themselves. Their eyes will dilate. They won't see a vampire. They won't see a person. All they'll see is food."

"So basically my siblings could be standing in front of me and not know me."

"Exactly."

"This is not a question of loyalty, it's a question of nature. Which means your ex-wife will be eaten alive by her own people."

"Fuck."

"Vampires usually go underground to prevent themselves from being sniffed out. Except for the ones who are chosen for The Fringale."

Cage sighed deeply.

"I have a special request." Anderson continued.

"Of course."

"I am available for everything you need. I will make sure that you are aware of our past, present and future history. In return I want only one thing. To be chosen for the battle of The Fringale. So that I can die as I wanted to many years ago now that I know the truth of the promise that we made to the Wolves will be out."

Silence.

Cage looked at him for what seemed like forever. Neither Cheddar nor Anderson knew what he was thinking.

Cheddar nudged him softly with his elbow. "You hear the man?"

"Oh...yeah. When it's time for the battle, I will choose you. I'll let you die."

By T. STYLES

PRESENT DAY

Tucked inside Violet's house, Kehinde stood in front of the bookshelf that was filled with Violet's grandmother's tales. He picked up one and looked at the hard cover.

Pierre's eyes never left him.

"She's so brilliant," Kehinde said holding the novel. "Truly the best of her time."

Violet approached, just to be near him. "She is. I love her so much. Not because she's a writer but because she's my Abuela."

He looked down at her with piercing eyes and her knees grew weak. "You will make her proud."

"Those are heavy words. Pierre said the same thing."

"I'm not sure about him, but as her editor, when I say you will make her proud, I want you to believe me. Especially with my help."

"Oh brother…" Pierre said, shaking his head.

Kehinde smiled at his dismay.

"Now, Violet, take me to what you have so far."

"Um…I…"

"She hasn't written a lot." Pierre interjected. "I mean, she has finished the first part of the last novel, but it still needs work."

Kehinde was annoyed every time he spoke. "Violet, show me what you have written."

"I'm going to be honest. Everything I have so far Pierre helped me with."

Kehinde shook his head and dragged a hand down his face. "What scenes?"

"Quite a few. Some scenes when the main character has to meet with The Elders and some more scenes when Cage's love interest begins to forget him."

Kehinde was heated. "Some scenes when his love interest forgets him. Fuck is the point of that?"

She looked at Pierre. "He thought it would be a good twist."

"I bet he did." He glared. "Well, I don't know about all that."

"Do I have to delete it all?"

"Is there a deadline?"

"Yes. My grandmother's lawyer sent it to me yesterday. I have to double check but I believe the deadline is in a couple of weeks."

Kehinde looked at Pierre. "We have work to do but I think your guest needs to leave. So we can focus."

By T. STYLES

"Nigga, I'm not going anywhere."

"Who are you exactly?" Kehinde said approaching, as if he didn't already know the answer. "Because for real, you seem shady."

"Who I am is none of your business." Pierre crossed his arms over his chest.

"And still I want to know."

"I'm someone who has been taking care of her and–.""

"Are you her brother?" Kehinde pressed.

Pierre's head tilted to the right. "No."

"Uncle? Cousin?"

"No." He said through clenched teeth.

"So you're a lover?" He pointed at him.

"No...he isn't. Not really I don't think so anyway." She tugged at her dress.

"So let me get this straight, a complete stranger comes into your home and you have given him the authority to write your grandmother's most prized tale? The finale to her series."

She looked downward.

"You're being a jerk," Pierre added. "Even if you are the editor, why be rude?"

"A jerk. Just because I told her the truth?"

"It's the way you do it!"

Kehinde smiled. "If it's tact that you want among other things," he side-eyed Violet's thin dress, "I'll leave you to it." He faced Violet completely. "But I am here to make sure this book exceeds your grandmother's wishes."

"I understand."

"We are beyond understanding now." Kehinde said. "I need to know; do you trust me?"

"She doesn't even know you to–."

Kehinde raised his hand to silence him. Looking into Violet's eyes, putting her into a soft trance he said, "Do you trust me?"

"Yes. Somehow I do."

"Then show me what you have."

Five minutes later Kehinde was reading over the book that was halfway written. He read an epic love story that was about a man and woman but also about three friends whose friendship was coming to an end. And he read many more things.

Looking at Pierre he glared. "Wow, looks like you really have Oignon getting his way in this tale."

"The book is named after him." Pierre said. "So I'd say he's the hero."

"Oignon," Kehinde said. "In French it means Onion."

By T. STYLES

Pierre glared. "It does."

"Well, this will never work," Kehinde opened a new document.

"Really?" Violet said, fingertips trembling over her lips.

"Really."

"But we've gotten so far."

"He didn't even give it a chance," Pierre continued.

"I'm still reading...but I will be honest, I'm going to erase what I think will destroy the brand and keep the rest."

"Can you tell me what makes it so bad?" Violet questioned.

"It's one sided," Kehinde said.

"Again, the book is called Oignon."

"I hear all that shit. For this to do your grandmother justice, we must make it more believable. After I finish reading, I'll tell you what's needed. All that other stuff, we will cut. For now...let me finish."

CHAPTER TWENTY-TWO
TATUM

They chose to eat under the full moon.

A large dining room table that sat twenty, with Tatum at the head, Row at the opposite and his uncles Canelo and Shannon spread out on one side, was the focal point. In front of them was a variety of food but the largest meal was that of meat so raw, they kept it on sponge like material to mop up the blood.

Also in attendance was Bloom and Flow who as he spoke, looked on at him in awe. Besides, he was a long way from what they remembered before Cage locked them away. Not only had his muscular frame filled out, just like Flow's, Tatum actually grew taller and above all more powerful.

After grabbing a piece of meat, Tatum wiped his mouth with the back of his hand. Standing up, he snatched a glass of red wine and huge drops splattered everywhere. "I'm excited today. As I look amongst all of you my heart is full. Because after what seemed like an eternity, finally my brother and sister have returned. This makes us stronger!"

Everyone cheered.

By T. STYLES

"And I realize that we are far from perfect. There are a lot of things happening with the pack that we must understand. But I want you to know that under my leadership I will make sure that I keep the women in our beds, fresh meat on the table and love for all of you in my heart."

More cheers.

Tatum focused on his siblings. "Flow, I can't imagine what you and Bloom went through. But I want you to realize that as surely as I stand here that we will make up for the lost time."

Flow looked at him and nodded. From everyone's perspective, it didn't seem that he was too excited about what was being said by his older brother. In fact if you looked at him close enough there appeared to be a hint of jealousy behind his eyes.

And although Tatum didn't see it, Shannon did.

"Do you have anything you want to say?" Tatum continued.

Flow took a deep breath. "What are we doing?"

"I don't understand the question, brother."

"I mean what are we doing? Where are you taking us? The vampires are growing at a large rate and yet we're here eating red meat and acting like suckers."

"Now is not the time for discussing business." Row said. "We are celebrating life."

"If not now than when?"

"Perhaps after we've had a chance to enjoy your homecoming." Tatum continued, slightly embarrassed.

"I'm home, now what?" He threw his arms up and let them drop back at his side.

A few people gasped.

"No disrespect, but let me worry about enjoying my homecoming. Bloom and I had a lot of time to think about this moment. About what would happen when we returned home. So while it's new to y'all, it's not to us. What I want now is activity."

"What does that look like for you?" Tatum questioned.

"You know what it looks like."

"Are you talking about revenge?"

Silence.

"We're waiting on an answer." Row said to Flow.

"If I am, what of it?"

"Revenge against who?" Tatum continued.

"Are we really going to play dumb? Just because Cage is my brother doesn't mean he shouldn't get what he deserves. He promised he'd never put us through what we went through when we were younger. And he

By T. STYLES

did it anyway. His own flesh and blood. And I want him to answer to it."

"And he will. Not right now." Tatum said it loudly. "Because there is much you don't understand. For starters, Cage is the reason Vamps and Wolves aren't fighting each other in the street now. He brings order. We need that."

"You know, I remember when you were weak. And instead of getting stronger I see you've gotten weaker over time. And that's disappointing."

"Flow, you're going too far!" Row said.

Flow pushed back his chair and rose. "Forgive me for destroying your meal but I'm out. It's too soft around here for me."

Bloom tugged at his hand but he pulled away.

After showering Flow jumped into his car and hit it to an address he still remembered. The moment he knocked on the door of an upscale brownstone, he was greeted with a hug when Gunnar appeared on the other side.

Gunnar and his pack were the first ones who agreed to follow Flow when he was charged with leading the Wolf pack. But due to Rue eating Vamps and Bloom's reckless behavior, Flow was removed from the throne and tucked away.

But with Tatum in power, he isolated Gunnar and his pack. He didn't like the rebel spirit they possessed and he also felt Gunnar was too loyal to Flow.

But that was then.

Now, Gunnar was excited and happy to see his rightful king. And he hoped he had a plan to get back on the throne.

After drinks and weed, the two friends caught up.

"It's not that I don't respect your brother's leadership." He placed his arm on the back of the sofa and sat back. "He didn't even give me a chance to follow him. Just kicked us out."

"He's weak. But I'll be different."

"Wait, you think you'll be in charge again?"

"I know I will. Especially when I convince everyone that Tatum doesn't have what it takes to make the tough decisions. And I bring them the vampire queen Angelina."

"That's going to be difficult. The leaders warm to him. They like his soft nature so turning them against him will be hard."

"I got a plan. Trust me. It may take a little time but it will work. First, I have to find my girl."

Gunnar nodded and looked down.

"Where is she, Gunnar? Where is Mink?"

"You know the rules. When you left she wasn't fresh anymore. The men only wanted to fuck her since her pussy formed to your dick. But she wouldn't let anyone touch her. And bounced."

Flow grinned. "That's my bitch. Where is she now?"

Silence.

"Gunnar, where is Mink?"

"With the vampire queen Angelina. Cage's ex-wife. She follows her now."

CHAPTER TWENTY-THREE
ANGELINA

Angelina was enjoying a cool night's run alone on a racing track. It was so important for her and her Linas to be fast that she poured the same energy into her own training. And when it came to her agility and quickness, she was queen.

She was pushing the limits of what was humanly possible, when suddenly someone caught up with her. The moment she saw Cage's face she stopped.

"If you're coming to me about that bitch we injected with D, don't. Or if you coming to me about the videos we sent out, I don't give a fuck. All of this shit is on you. I told you not to betray me."

He glared. "Fuck are you planning?" He said with all seriousness.

"I don't know what you're talking about." She grinned.

"You've been too quiet. I don't trust you."

"Let me get this straight, you tell me to fall back and I do. And even now you think something is up? You even had the bloggers thinking I was crazy." She grinned. "You won. Be happy."

By T. STYLES

Cage stepped closer. "Listen, the Wolves will never, ever be your people. There will come a time where they will be forced to choose. And trust me, they won't choose you."

Angelina walked away and returned. "You don't know anything about my family."

"Again, they aren't your family."

"They are to me." She pointed to herself. "And you destroyed them at that party! You destroyed me too."

Cage wanted to tell her everything he knew. About 'The Cravings' and the battle at 'The Fringale'. And how even Wolves that cared about vampires would not be able to resist during that time.

And that included his siblings.

But he couldn't trust her.

And it was mostly his fault.

"I need you to understand something, I will continue to do what I want to in life, Cage. And ain't shit you can do about it."

"You're being selfish."

She shook her head and tossed her arms up. "Call it what you want. I can't believe I'm even listening to you. It's not like we've ever had a serious relationship."

He frowned. "Fuck are you talking about?"

"What we had was brief. And...fleeting. Outside of you being the leader of The Collective, we have nothing at all."

"Angelina, I realize you're mad but why you faking like you don't remember our past?"

Silence.

"Angelina, why the fucking games?"

After a few more minutes it became obvious. She wasn't lying. She was looking at a man she was beginning to forget and for some reason it tore him apart inside.

Was this some sort of side effect from turning vampire?

And if so, why hadn't he suffered the same effects? Because despite being angry with her and her actions, every part of him missed her and longed to be with her again.

And yet, in the moment, he had to be stern.

"Angelina, you have to stop what you're doing." He moved closer. "It's getting to a point where I can't keep you safe anymore. That I...I can't prevent a blood bounty from being placed on your head."

"Are you threatening me again? Because you know how I handle threats. The more I get, the more dangerous I become."

By T. STYLES

"Do you understand what I'm saying?"

"Yes."

"Then why you smiling?"

She grinned brighter and ran away.

Angelina looked at her son who was strikingly handsome. He was running on a treadmill and despite pushing his body to the limit, he had yet to sweat. After all, vampires rarely produced the same body effects as Norms.

"Mother, why are you looking at me like that?"

She smiled. "I can't look at you now?"

"You can. But you have this look sometimes that makes me feel like you're thinking of something else. Or that you're afraid something will happen to me."

"I'm your mother. I'm right to worry."

"What's on your mind, ma?"

"Faster."

He increased the speed. "Are you going to continue to ignore me or answer the question?"

The treadmill was going so fast now had he been human he would have fallen off or suffered from a heart attack. But Godric ran as smooth as if he were taking a brisk walk around the block.

"I get that you're starting to get annoyed by me not allowing you to explore the world. And I understand my long gazes on you make you uncomfortable. But you can't tell a mother how to love. Or how to protect."

"Stop telling me something I already know."

"Then what do you want to-"

"I thought you were letting me meet my father. Who is he? As a man."

Angelina frowned.

"Mother, tell me more about my father."

"Godric, not right-."

"Why is it that every time I try to talk to you about him, it's blocked out?"

"I...I...don't know." She paused and took a deep breath. "Godric, when I spoke to you about him before, where did I say we met?"

"Wait, are you serious?"

Silence.

He continued to run. "You told me before that his name is Cage and that you met as kids."

"Really? I've known him that long?"

By T. STYLES

"Yes. But lately when I want more you say you can't remember details. Did he hurt you that badly? That you block him out this way. Do I have to introduce myself to him for disrespecting my-."

"No! Never…ever approach the king! Ever!"

He looked down. "Well, I have a right to know more about the man." He jumped off the treadmill, cut it off and walked over to her. "Did something happen recently between you two?"

She sat down. "Last night the vampire king visited me. And it's true, I am starting to forget things. But when I look at him and when I look at you, I feel something in here." She touched her chest. "I don't know if it's dementia or…"

"I'm sorry, ma. I thought you were being distant."

"It's okay." She squeezed his hand. "So when you ask me about him it's not that I'm hiding anything. I don't remember."

There was a knock at the door.

"Come inside." Angelina said softly.

Carmen walked into the room. "Godric, can I speak to your mother alone?"

"Of course." He kissed Angelina on the cheek and then kissed Carmen before leaving.

"What do you want? You know I need time with my son. With him growing at the rate he's been, he's starting to ask a lot of questions."

"I want to tell you something. And I don't want you to get mad." She paused. "Mink's Wolves hover over us during the day. I think they're mad that you let Cage get away. The night we lost the Minks and the Linas."

"She isn't holding grudges." She frowned. "How do you even know they hover? You aren't awake."

"I can smell them when the moon is high and I open my eyes. They look over us and I'm afraid. I swear it!"

Angelina rose and moved close to her. For some reason what Cage said played in her mind. "I trust Mink and her Wolves with my life."

"And you may have to." Carmen stepped closer. "But I don't. I mean, we brush off the whole Wolves eating vampire shit because they roll with us on the streets. But what happens when they crave the taste and can't find a vampire? How do you know they won't turn on us? And why is this even happening in the first place? I don't think we thought enough about why they like eating vampire so much."

"You're right. I haven't." Angelina took a deep breath. "So what's your plan?"

"We need Day Walkers to protect us when we're asleep. We need Day Walkers to protect us from Mink and her Wolves. And we need them now."

Angelina took a deep breath. "Okay."

Carmen sighed deeply. "I'll take care of everything."

Angelina smiled. "Look, keep this away from-."

"Mink...I know." Carmen said finishing her sentence. "I don't want to hurt her feelings either. But this is the right thing to do."

Angelina took a deep breath. "In the meantime, did you get the news anchor and her cameraman?"

"Yes. They're afraid but like you suggested I promised not to hurt them if they do what we want. Even though their blood smells so sweet."

"Good...since Cage paid bloggers to convince everyone that the sightings at the movie theater were a hoax, it's time to take it up another notch. Let's proceed with the plan."

Later on that night Angelina and her Linas took to the streets with a news anchor and her cameraman filming it all. They bit strangers on the necks out in the open. They showed up at events and allowed their fangs to drop in full view. They stayed away from clubs, since the Mag's were present, but they went everywhere else.

In more than all of the cases, they allowed onlookers to record.

It was a bloody massacre filled night.

When she was done, tucked in the backseat of her car, with the cameraman filming and her mouth dripping red with blood, she said, "Okay, Cage. You want to threaten me again? Because I can do more."

Officer Oscar James and Larry Parker looked through the interrogation room glass window at the news anchor and her cameraman who sat shaken as they gave their testimonies. Both covered in blood.

"You heard what she said right?" Oscar asked Larry. "The woman in the video mentioned Cage again. We should have taken him in when we had the chance."

The officers had been to Cage's home before after accounts of women being bitten ran through the city. But because they didn't have anything to hold him on, they let him go. And now, once again, his name was coming up in the mix.

p3

p4

p5

p6

p7

p8

p9

p10

216   By T. STYLES

But this time they were determined to do something about it.

All night they went through the streets paying close attention to places with limited lighting. That included clubs, movie theaters and bowling alleys.

When they didn't see anything out of the ordinary, they happened upon a young man who looked as if he could be a model, speaking closely to a female who was smiling so wide they thought her face would crack. They would've left him alone, but in the video every vampire, every single one, was strikingly handsome.

This person included.

"Pull over. I want to see what's going on." Oscar said to Larry.

"So what are you two getting into tonight?" Oscar asked, standing over the couple.

"Why you asking?" Brian, who happened to be one of the members of Onion's Collection, questioned.

The girl took off running.

"She didn't seem too happy." Oscar said. "That's okay. We'll take you out."

"What you saying?" Brian snapped.

Oscar grabbed his arm. "You're coming with me."

Larry looked at Oscar in confusion. There was no law that said a person couldn't be speaking to another one on the streets. So he had no idea where his partner was going.

At first, Brian was calm in the back of the squad car as they drove. Larry asked Brian limited questions, but Oscar seemed more interested in driving long enough to let the sun come up. And as Larry looked through the rear-view mirror he saw Brian who was once calm was now uneasy and staring back.

"You're playing with your life." Brian said out of nowhere.

Larry glared. "What did you just say to me?"

"You heard me. Let me out now or else."

"Or else what?" Oscar said with disdain. "Are you afraid of the sun? Are you–."

Suddenly the car was struck from the left. Once hit, the vehicle spun a few times before being struck from the right. Within seconds the car doors were being ripped off by two people.

Both Larry and Oscar sat wide-eyed and in horror as they looked at the unusual strength from both a woman and a man who once again, looked like models.

Not too far away, a van with blacked out windows sat with the engine running. Waiting. The officers couldn't see inside.

By T. STYLES

When Brian was free from the squad car he walked up to the window. The couple who freed him stood behind him. Leaning down he said, "You can try and find me. You can even ask a lot of questions. But ask yourself this first, is it worth it?" He smiled. "I mean, do you really wanna die?"

He dropped his fangs and both Larry and Oscar screamed loudly.

Brian walked calmly to the van with the duo following behind him as they sped out of sight.

Sitting in their car which was now smoking Larry said, "It's true."

"It's fucking true."

"What do we do now?" Larry continued.

"We bring this shit to light."

The Elders sat in awe and rage as they looked at their truth being played out on national television. As of the moment it was still considered a hoax, but they all knew this wouldn't last.

"I want them niggas dead!" Marco yelled, slamming his fist into the table.

"Who?" An Elder asked.

"Cage! Angelina! Onion! All of them! Now!"

LANGLEY

Cage was furious as he sat in his lounge with various members of his Collection after seeing the videos and hearing that the news anchor and the cameraman blabbed to the police.

Langley stood next to him.

"The news?" He whispered. "How the fuck can I spin this?"

Standing up, he paced with his fangs hung as he looked at video after video of the disrespect.

"Sir, what do you want me to do about her?" Langley asked.

Cage flopped in his chair. A hand dragged down his face. "You know, she claims to be forgetting me? When

By T. STYLES

I caught up with her and warned her about doing shit like this."

Helena glared. "She's just mad. Mad you chose me. Mad you chose us."

"Could be true." His head dropped back and forward again. "But somehow I think it's something else." He pointed at her.

"Like what?" Langley asked.

"When I looked into her eyes, I saw a blank slate. And back in the day, Onion said something to me about rewriting life and...I don't know but I think that has something to do with it."

"Sir, we have to make a decision on her. Before Norms find out we're real and start seeking us out."

"I KNOW!" Cage roared.

They cowered under his might.

"I...I know what we have to do." He said softer. "In the meantime, I'll make a few calls to spin the stories going around on television. Right now it appears to be speculation but between Daylight and Angelina...shit getting tight."

"Sir, why...why did you let Dickens go the night he came to the club?"

He sighed. "Because he's a man of honor. Fighting for his people. Like I'm fighting for mine."

Langley nodded. "Shane and Ellis are coming back to town in a couple of days to see how they can help."

Cage nodded. "I hate to keep using them. Since they handled the Viking shit but...I may have to lean on them a bit more."

Langley nodded. "Sir, we have a plan too." He looked at the members in his Collection. "If you want to hear it."

"I know what you're going to say. I have to kill her. And it's true. But don't make a move until I give the okay. Is that understood?"

Langley nodded yes although he was eager to get revenge for what she did to his Candy.

By T. STYLES

CHAPTER TWENTY-FOUR
ROW

I t was a celebration.

Earlier in the day Row had wed his new bride. And as a result, it was time to party which everyone was looking forward to. Music, food, and joy flooded the event as all did their best to welcome the new couple.

Bloom was also in attendance.

Flow was not.

Everyone was having a good time until...the atmosphere changed.

The thing was, not too far from the party, across the park, vampires gathered after recently being converted. They weren't necessarily within eyesight of the Wolves but...well...suddenly they could smell them. When a breeze carrying their odor continued to draft toward Row's celebration, Row who was dancing with his wife stopped in place.

"What is...that...delicious smell?" He asked.

Suddenly the rest of the Wolves stopped too. To be clear, they could smell vampires in the past, but never *like this*.

"I smell it too," Canelo said.

"Me...me too," Shannon responded.

"What...what is it?" Someone called out.

"I don't know!" Another said.

"But I want to have a piece," the new bride said looking up at Row. "I...I want to have it now. Can I?"

Tatum's muscles buckled as he took in the delicious aroma. "I've...I've never smelled anything so sweet."

Slowly Bloom stood up. "May I speak brother?"

Tatum looked at her. "What is this about?"

"Please."

He nodded.

"This is what I was locked away by Cage for." She said, trying not to salivate as the smell grew stronger.

"What does that mean?" Tatum asked.

"What you smell, right now, I smelled all my life. Whenever our brother was around. But now it's getting stronger, and I can't resist. More than anything I don't want to. And I have a feeling you won't be able to either."

Tatum remembered the look on Cage's face when he explained why he put them away. Could this be the real reason? "Let's talk about this later. In fact, maybe we should leave, Row. That way we can–"

"No. Let's talk about it now." Someone called out.

"She knows something and we have a right to know too!" Another yelled.

"I'm the leader!" Tatum roared. "You don't tell me what you want. I tell you!"

Row stepped up to him and placed a hand on his shoulder. "We can't run away from it anymore. Let her speak."

Tatum took a deep breath.

Looking out amongst the wedding party he said, "I don't know what my sister is about to say but I have a feeling it will change everything. And because of that I want to make clear that no one is authorized to make a move on vampires."

They nodded with understanding.

He was trying to keep his promise to Cage to prevent a war.

He looked at his sister and said, "Continue."

"Like I mentioned earlier, I've smelled this fragrance from the beginning. With Cage. And it was so great that it was hard to resist. It wasn't until I spent time locked away with Flow that I realized that maybe I wasn't alone. Sure I knew Rue felt the same way, but I didn't have any idea others felt it too. And I could be wrong but I believe we're having this craving for a reason."

Tatum looked at his uncles who were glued onto her every word.

"Just like the other beasts in the wild, maybe we're here for the circle of life. And maybe we shouldn't run from our natural inclinations. I won't do it any longer. Because I am fully aware that this thing that lives in me must serve a purpose. Because I'm not a bad person. And neither are you!" She continued.

Everyone grew excited.

"Be careful, Bloom." Tatum said. "We don't want a war."

"I am being careful, brother. Because if I told our people how sweet they taste…it would be total anarchy. And I don't want that under your reign." She whispered.

He glared.

"All I'm saying is I think things will get worse. And I think there will come a time, where we will no longer be able to deny that which rises in us. And maybe we should make room for that. Instead of fighting the feeling."

Luckily within an hour of her speech the vampires who were not too far away left after getting wind that Wolves were in the territory.

"So other than the circle of life, why do you think this is going on?" A Wolf asked.

"I think we are put here to save humans. From Vamps. Doesn't that make us saints? So why shouldn't we eat?"

CHAPTER TWENTY-FIVE
CAGE

S hit was getting thick for Cage and The Stryker Collection...

To ease the tension, they decided to go to the beach because he prevented his own from going to clubs or any place where they could be harmed. The only Brightside was that while most vampires preferred the nightlife, Cage and his Collection enjoyed being in nature. In addition, at the moment, they had the entire place to themselves.

It was serene.

"Are you okay?" Helena questioned, walking up behind him.

He sighed. "Why do you always do that? You see I'm enjoying my privacy but you press me anyway."

She took a deep breath. "Lately you've gotten so fickle. If I ignore you totally you would think something would be wrong–."

"Yes, you have a duty to see about me. But asking me what's wrong every five minutes is starting to get old."

"Then what should I say, Cage?"

"Ask me how you can be helpful."

She smiled as if suddenly getting what he was saying. "Okay, how can I be helpful?"

"I've decided to kill Angelina."

She nodded and tried to keep a neutral face. "I think it's a good choice."

"I'm sure you do."

"Don't be that way, Cage. I don't like her but she's still a vampire. And I don't want to see any of our people hurt. But she's left you no choice."

"This conversation is going nowhere."

She waved her arms back and forth. "You know I don't lie to you. And I hear what you say, about ridding us of Angelina. But even prior to now, some think you won't be able to follow through. I mean I know you mean well but can you actually pull the-."

"Of course there will be pause. This isn't just another woman."

"As opposed to me?"

"Exactly."

She lowered her head and then looked at him squarely in the eyes. "I know you said it to be mean but I'm listening all the same."

"She was my wife. And so yes, I do have a problem pushing through. But it doesn't mean I won't do it when the time is right."

Suddenly someone rushed in their direction and entered the ocean. It was so quick the person appeared as a blur. Before Cage could understand what was happening more figures rushed towards the ocean.

Within seconds, he witnessed a fight that was occurring between several members of his Collection and what appeared to be male Wolves. Most were wearing gray sweatpants and no shirt.

Just their presence made his skin run cold.

They were being attacked.

One on one mostly, but still enough to do damage.

Helena and Cage quickly joined the battle. The Wolves bit and the vampires hit, pushed, and shoved. If this was an example of what was to occur during the battle at The Fringale, Cage knew it would be brutal.

But *his* wasn't an ordinary Collection.

They were strong.

Vicious.

Cage and his family slammed Wolves into the water repeatedly, making them dizzy and off balance. If only it had been a full moon the fight could've been over sooner.

By T. STYLES

But it wasn't. And so he would have to rely on his God-given strength to save himself and his crew.

Fangs were dropped and muscles popped as the fist fight went well into the evening. It was obvious that no one could win as things continued. Realizing this, Cage raised his hand. "Stop!"

The blood bath continued.

"I said stop!!"

The fighting got stronger.

"STOP NOW!"

Suddenly the Wolves and Vamps looked upon him.

He took a deep breath. "We can be here forever, Wolves. But unless you are willing to give your lives," he focused on the shirtless men, "which we are fully prepared to take, it's best that you leave now and live to fight another day."

"Why should we care? If we continue to fight, the sun will shine and you will be caught under its light. I prefer my meat raw. But I'll take it cooked too."

Cage glared. "True. If we continue, the sun will rise. But what do you think we will do in the meantime? Fight less or harder? So to prevent all of that, isn't it smarter to leave now?"

The Wolves saw the strength in the vampire's eyes. They could see they were prepared to go the distance.

But what they also saw was something different. They would survive not only to protect themselves.

But to protect Cage.

The pack leader said, "We will conclude tonight."

As they left the water Cage said, "Who sent you?"

As he waited for his answer he prayed it wasn't his brother Tatum.

"Your own people. The ones who lived the longest."

"The Elders." Cage said to himself.

"Yes. But it doesn't matter. Because we are aware now who we are. We are aware that you are nothing more than fruit for our picking. So if it's not us, another pack will come soon. Maybe all of you should say your goodbyes while you still can."

The Stryker Collection stood in front of him as their skin began to heal on sight.

The battle had begun.

CHAPTER TWENTY-SIX
CAGE

A breeze washed over Cheddar's property as he and Cage stood on the deck of his home. Cage was pacing back and forth and was so angry he had yet to put up his fangs.

"It's starting," Cage said passionately. "It's fucking starting. You should have seen how they attacked us. Had it been a different Collection, these niggas would've taken us out."

"Like they did a chunk of my people, and Onion's also. Although Onion's Collection being unprepared is not surprising seeing as how they continue to put themselves in harm's way."

"Exactly. But we not out there in the streets. We in nature! Fuck wrong with these old ass niggas?!" He continued to pace. "They said it was The Elders." He stopped in front of him. "It was an orchestrated attack."

"It could definitely be them. We know what they're capable of. But are you sure it wasn't Tatum? After all, you did snatch Bloom and Flow. Told me yourself. Maybe it's revenge."

Cage frowned. "You don't know what you talking about."

"Listen, we aren't friends."

"That much is true. That doesn't mean you need to be disrespectful."

"And it's not my intent. But everyone knows you have Wolf brothers and a sister. And many people think that you will let them get away with whatever they want. Maybe they're starting by getting rid of you. How do we know they aren't–."

"I'm not speaking on my family or my ex-wife anymore at this point."

Cheddar took a deep breath. "What about the percentage?"

"What about it?"

"You're seeing the effects of not making a decision. You have to decide who will go to The Fringale. And you have to do it now."

"The fucking Elders are going! They up! I just have to find out how to get them there. They're too strong and won't go on their own."

"Agreed."

Cage looked down and up at him. "But...but based on The Elder attack I need...we need Angelina and her Linas. For now anyway."

"That makes no sense!"

"You didn't see what I saw. With the Wolves!"

"I don't need to. By Angelina allowing the Minks to eat flesh before the clock has dinged, more Wolves would get the impression that they can do it too. It's open season on us. Instead of getting her help, kill her. Then the rest will fall."

"I know you have heard the saying hell has no fury as a woman scorned."

Cheddar nodded.

"I have a plan and I'd like to use her Wolves. After that I'm done."

"Even if I want to believe it, how can we use them? They can't be controlled."

"It's a numbers game. I have access to a few of Tatum's Wolves, but Tatum is starting to get tired of going against the pack. But since the female Wolves are on Angelina's side, this gives us more numbers."

"Do you trust me?"

"Cheddar, stop the games. Shit's about to pop off now."

"I'm serious. Do you trust me? Because Onion didn't. And it made our relationship a struggle."

"I trust you. Because most of The Collective remembers the relationship you had with Tino. And I need men like that on my side."

"You mean your father?"

"That man was no father of mine."

He chuckled. "But still, you have his blood. And it's the only reason why people listen to you. But if you go talking that Angelina's Wolves shit, you'll undo everything. She's too messy. Caused too many problems. Don't mix your story with hers."

Cage nodded although he would do what he willed. "Where's Onion? Lately he's been missing. And I don't want him returning and fucking everything up."

He took a deep breath. "I...I don't know."

"It seems odd that the world is falling apart and he's nowhere to be found."

"He's a non-factor, Cage. He hasn't been organized. Ever." He paused. "My focus is now on you and keeping you safe. While his is on...well...Angelina."

CHAPTER TWENTY-SEVEN
CAGE

Cage sat in the car outside of the graveyard for hours...

It had been years since he visited his parents' grave. Per his mother's request, they had been buried next to one another. And now that he was there, he felt like he wanted to bounce. Besides the guilt that he felt upon being responsible for their demise, due to the men who killed his mother trying to get at him instead, coupled with Onion murdering Magnus, weighed on him.

But he needed their energy.

Because it was possible that in a matter of months, he would be at war with his flesh and blood. And despite being dead, he wished his parents, especially his father could help him now.

Easing out of the car, he walked past the many gravesites of people gone on. Before long, he happened upon their graves. Taking a deep breath he said, "Hey, ma. Hey, dad."

An owl hooted in the distance.

"I don't know if you can see what's going on, but things are getting bad. The thing is I know I made a promise to you, to protect Tatum, Flow and Bloom. And I'm trying. I really am. But shit..."

He shuffled a little.

"Shit may not go as planned. And I want you to know I'm going to do all I can to avoid it. But I don't know if it will work."

Suddenly he smelled rain.

Shaking his head he said, "What are you doing here?"

Onion stepped up next to him. "How do you do that?"

"What do you want? Because the last thing I want to be doing is talking to the man who killed my father over his grave."

"I mean no disrespect."

"Then make it quick and get the fuck out of here."

"I heard you been looking for me."

He nodded. "By who? Cheddar?"

He frowned. "You still talking to that nigga?"

So it wasn't Cheddar. Cage thought.

"I wasn't looking for you. But I noticed you been missing in action lately. If you gonna stay away that's fine. But whatever you do, don't get in the way of my plans."

"The Elders sent Wolves after my men again last night. That's twice in a row. They ate half of they asses up. I kicked rocks. I ain't got but twenty men left."

"You a stupid ass nigga." He shrugged. "But why you telling me?"

"They fucking shit up, Cage."

"Again, why are you telling me?"

"I want to call a Truce."

"That's not what you really want. So stop wasting my time and get to the point."

"I want to band together and fight these Wolves. We have to."

Cage nodded. "With twenty niggas?"

"It's better than none."

"Why should I trust you? You show up at my parents' grave. Disrespect. Sound stupid. Get all of your men chewed. I mean for real, why would I unite with that?"

"Fuck all that dumb shit, nigga! Will you work with me? We can always get back to beefing later. Every second counts."

"A little while ago I met Angelina on the racetrack, and she didn't recognize me. Do you know why?"

He smiled. "Nah."

Cage felt he was lying. "I don't believe you." He paused. "Just so you know, if she can get some sense, I want her back."

Onion shook his head. "Then that makes us enemies. Because I want her too."

"At least I know where you're coming from now." Cage took a deep breath. "For the moment, we'll call a truce. Plus, I have a plan."

"I'm listening."

"It involves Angelina."

"I'm not surprised." Onion responded.

CHAPTER TWENTY-EIGHT
CAGE

Cage sat with Onion in an apartment within the building that Onion bought for Angelina. It was the building where Onion threatened her life due to being unfaithful with Cage when they were younger.

Now Angelina, her Linas and her Wolves occupied it freely.

Sitting in the living room with her Linas behind her, she waited eagerly to see what Onion wanted. The Wolves were notably left out of the meeting since the conversation involved them. But it didn't mean she wouldn't tell them later.

She wasn't the only person who brought members of their Collections. Cage had his Collection behind him as well as what was left of Onion's Collection. In a sense, all were saying no one trusted the other.

"Things are getting bad." Cage started.

"I'm waiting on the part that has to do with me."

"We need you to join us. At least until we can come to a truce." Onion said. "I explained that to you when you agreed to have this meeting with me."

She shook her head. "The Elders haven't done shit to me. Just you and your vampire king as he's known around here."

Carmen frowned. Up until this point she thought Angelina was blocking him out as a way to deal with her pain. But now she realized something more sinister was going on. Her queen honestly appeared to be suffering memory loss. And if that was true, what were they fighting for?

Cage frowned. "Are we still doing this?" He asked Angelina. "Are we still playing this fucking game?"

"What are you talking about?" Angelina glared.

"You spent your life with me! Why all of a sudden don't you remember?" He paused. "Not only that but you have a child with me too."

"How do you know about my son?"

Cage's heart thumped. "Your son is of my blood. How would that happen if we don't know each other?"

She glared. "You're a fucking liar."

Cage didn't want to talk about their personal business. Shit hurt too much anyway. But he really needed to reach her now. "If not me then who?"

"You run up on me. You threatened me and –."

"When I ran up on you I asked you not to go against your own people! It wasn't to threaten you!"

By T. STYLES

"Angelina, my darling." Onion interrupted.

Before Cage's eyes, he saw her face soften when she looked at him. "Yes, Onion."

"Can you hear me out if you won't listen to Cage?"

She nodded. "Speak."

"Things are changing. And we don't want to come back to this moment when we had the chance to do something and didn't."

"This is not my problem. This is not my war."

"*Now*!" Onion said. "This is not your war *now*. But it can be when shit gets out of hand. How do you know The Elders won't hit you soon? And have you killed in your sleep? May even use your own Wolves against you."

"She doesn't know," Cage said.

Carmen whispered in her ear, angering both Cage and Onion. When she was done Angelina said, "This meeting is over."

Cage tossed his body back. "Why?"

"You're trying to sow doubt in my camp."

"This will be a big mistake," Onion said.

"Maybe...but we'll never know."

When Cage and Onion were outside, Cage stepped to him. "What is going on with her?"

Onion smiled. "What you mean? She said no. It's over."

"Why is she still pretending not to know me? Are you playing games? Is it seduction or something?"

Onion took a deep breath. "Trying to understand why she's doing what she's doing is a waste of time. Time better spent preparing for war against The Elders. Who you wronged. Not everybody loves you, Cage. Some folks want you dead."

"It sounds like you're threatening me."

"I'm telling you to be cautious."

"I'm always prepared. Just so you know, I got a plan nobody will see coming. So I'm good."

CHAPTER TWENTY-NINE
THE ELDERS

M arco stood before The Elders draped in a red velvet robe with nothing underneath.

He was still fuming after learning that Viking had been murdered. And for the first time in their vampire lives The Elders were realizing that maybe it would be their time to die on the field of The Fringale after all.

But in Marco's opinion it wouldn't go down without a fight. "I still can't believe that Cage and his friends are causing so much strife. The blogs, the news and now even the cops, are all talking about us! But the way they did Viking, by dragging him out into the sun like a low-level vampire is unforgivable! How could they be so disrespectful?"

Paris stepped up. "We should have involved him more in the percentage process. Instead of going behind his back."

"But that would have meant one or many of us would have to die. Isn't that the purpose of using him in the first place? To hide the truth."

Paris took a deep breath. "We have spoken before of the lottery system. Let's go back to–"

"No, Paris you talked about the lottery system." He pointed at him. "I always said no."

In the past, the lottery system was shot down because it would mean pulling numbers from The Elders. This meant everyone was given a ticket exactly six days before the battle at The Fringale who were two hundred years or older. Elders would then attend an event where numbers would be called. If your number was called, you'd say your goodbyes to your family and report to the battle.

Which almost always ended in death.

"Cage is not falling for the games anymore." Paris said. "He doesn't want to be a part of *our* plan. So that means we have to come up with another. Are you doing that or are you more interested in crying over the loss of Viking?"

"I have some ideas." Marco responded. "It's what I wanted to talk to you about."

The Elders breathed a sigh of relief. Because it was known that both Viking and Marco were good when it came to coming up with a way out. And they needed one now.

"Well what is it?" Paris asked.

"Since Cage disrespectfully killed Arabia and Viking, in scenarios that brought them no honor, we have to let him see the error of his ways."

"I'm waiting on details." Paris persisted.

"Sending the Wolves didn't work. For Onion, Cheddar or Cage's Collections."

"Again, tell us something new!"

"Instead of using Wolves, I say we kill them in their sleep. So I hired a group of Day Walkers. Like they did with us."

"So you involved other vampires?" Paris questioned. "Are you stupid or dumb?"

"First off they aren't vampires if they haven't taken The Fluid."

"Marco, we can't let people know that we are publicly on the opposite end of killing Tino's son." Another Elder said. "That's why we sent Wolves in the first place."

"The boy left me no choice."

"That's just it, he's a man!" Paris said. "And had we treated him like one and told the truth, shit would not have gotten out of control."

The sun was high, and Cage and his Collection were asleep in their rooms behind locked doors. There was a quiet hush over his estate and birds could be heard chirping and singing in the distance.

Just like Marco intended, slowly the hired Day Walkers ascended on Cage's property. They were fifty deep, which meant unless there was an army at his house, Cage and the Stryker Collection would meet their demise that morning.

Once reaching the property, Kiera, who was in charge, looked at the men under her deployment. "Go around the back and cover all doors." She pointed.

They dispatched per her orders.

Then she looked at Jefferson. "Take the side of the house."

"We're on it!"

"Your group take the side," She said to Vincent's group.

When everyone had their orders, she went toward the front of the house with ten men. The plan was to kick

By T. STYLES

the door down when suddenly it opened and a single man appeared.

A Norm at that.

She wasn't taken aback. At the end of the day, it was Cage Stryker, so she knew he had security. But what shocked her was how his body smelled. Although she was a Day Walker, she could still detect the slight odor that Norms gave from their blood.

And this person smelled of chocolate chip cookies.

"Hello." His response was simple.

"Who are you?" She asked, arms wrapped behind her back.

"Since you're on private property, I think the better question would be who are you?"

She smiled. "I must say, I hadn't expected Cage to entrust a human with his security. But I like it. At the same time, it won't stop us from getting inside."

He shrugged. "Maybe. Or maybe not."

"You interest me." She pointed at him.

"I'm glad I amuse you. But you have under five minutes to get off of this property."

"Why should we leave? We like it here."

"Understood." He nodded. "Mr. Stryker does have a stunning estate. I was taken aback when I first saw it myself."

"Oh, so you are a fan?"

"Technically I would be considered an enemy."

She laughed. "Oh, you must tell me who you are now." She giggled louder. It was one thing to deal with a Norm but to learn that he also hired an enemy. "The suspense is killing me."

Suddenly the sets of men she dissipated around several areas of the property walked toward the center with their arms raised. Guns were upon them by men dressed similarly to the one standing before her.

"Cookie, cookie, cookie," she laughed, while looking at him. "I underestimated Cage. And I underestimated you too."

The Norm smiled and grew serious. "Please leave the property." Guns clicked from everywhere. "Or we'll shoot. Starting with you."

Kiera nodded and slowly turned around.

Her entourage followed.

Sitting in the dining room, Dickens and eight members of his activist group Daylight sat with Cage in

By T. STYLES

his home. Cage was posted at the head of his table with members of the Stryker Collection on his right.

Cage gambled majorly by trusting him.

And it paid off.

The alliance that he made with the Daylight activists first had to be explained to his own Collection before inviting Dickens and his members over.

He had to tell the Strykers the truth.

The COMPLETE truth.

He told them about The Elders.

He told them about the battle at The Fringale.

He told them about The Cravings.

He watched their eyes grow sad upon realizing that unlike they were told in the past, they actually wouldn't live forever. In the end, they were grateful because they would make the next few hundred years count as long as Cage remained their leader. Because as they were learning, they didn't have always.

When Cage was clear with his Collection, he explained his need to meet the Daylight's. Although the Daylight's were his sworn enemy, wanting to kill vampires, meeting them had mutual benefits.

But Cage was smart.

This wasn't an overnight plan.

Before approaching Dickens, Cage investigated him from afar. He saw the kind of man he was and he watched those he was in connection with in life. Just like himself, Dickens was very selective of those in his company and Cage admired this trait.

Another reason he trusted Dickens was because he felt it was time to take a chance. Very soon the secret would be out to the world that Vampires and Wolves were real. That The Cravings could cause a war on the street.

And so it was best to get out ahead of it all.

Besides, he couldn't control Angelina and her Linas who were intent on acting out in public. By opening up to the Daylight's, first, he showed he also had a moral compass.

Third, Cage explained to the Daylight's the purpose of the Vamps and Wolves. And how that at some point Wolves would ensure Vampires don't overpopulate. And so despite the darkness of the moment, humanity's God had provided a way into the light. And that Cage, for as long as he reigned, would ensure a percentage would meet their demise, thereby ensuring the existence of mankind.

Upon hearing the details, which he believed, Dickens quickly learned that without Cage, Norms would perish in great numbers. Because vampire or not, Cage had a code.

In other words, Dickens needed Cage.

And Cage needed Dickens.

Upon the recollection that he wasn't losing his mind, that vampires were real, Dickens liked Cage immediately due to his honesty.

And despite the intoxicating smell of Dickens' blood, which meant he had exposed weaknesses, Cage liked him too.

Speaking on the events of the morning, Dickens went on to explain how Day Walkers showed up at Cage's property as he slept. And how they meant to cause him great harm, even death. And how with his 500 men, only those he trusted the most, Dickens was able to fend them off. Although of the 500, only eight knew Cage was a vampire.

"I know this won't be the end. But I truly appreciate your help."

"Do you know who it was?" Dickens asked. "That tried to kill you?"

"I have some ideas."

"So when does this battle begin?" Dickens questioned.

"I'm not going to share that with you. Because while I believe you are a man of integrity these matters may place you at great risk."

"But you trusted me with your lives. While you slept."

"Because I had it on good authority that they would come tonight. Because there are members who realize it's their time to go and they don't want to." Cage thought of Paris, and how grateful he was for his call. "I needed your help."

"You won't be living here anymore, will you? In this house?"

"You mean now that you know my address?" Cage laughed.

He shook his head with a smile.

"No. I've been building a property off the grid for years. It's ready."

"Vampires?" Dickens whispered.

Silence.

"But I truly appreciate your help. And I wanted to meet you to let you know that you aren't crazy. You are very aware. You are very right. We are real. We are dangerous."

"I don't wish for accolades."

"That's why I trust you."

"But I have to warn you. You must stop the public protests. Other vampires won't waste time. They will kill you without hesitation."

"I'm not afraid." He sighed. "I have a duty to the Norms as you call us. I hope you understand."

"I do. I'm in the same shoes. May we meet in the streets."

Angelina, The Linas, Mink and her Wolves were speeding around the racetrack. When suddenly two cars pulled up and tossed tire spikes on the track. Because they were riding motorcycles, they couldn't stop in time and four Minks lost control of their bikes, followed by three Linas.

Angelina's eyes widened when eight Wolves exited the cars. They were all male and she could see by the look in their eyes that they were evil.

"Fight!" Angelina yelled.

On command, The Linas and the Minks charged the Wolves. Since it was fifteen Minks and twenty Linas, they doubled teamed the Wolves with their skills. It was a brutal fight that the Linas were starting to lose.

Concerned, Mink grabbed Angelina from the melee.

"GET OFF OF ME!" She yelled trying to get back.

"YOU HAVE TO LEAVE! THEY ARE WITH THE ELDERS AND THEY WANT YOU!"

"But they-."

"NOW!" Mink yelled. "We will be victorious. But not if we have to worry about you."

Tears rolled down Angelina's face. "I...I can't abandon you."

"It's not abandonment. We can't focus if we worry about you. I can't focus. Please my queen! Go!"

Angelina, realizing Mink spoke from the heart, ran away to safety.

CHAPTER THIRTY
CAGE

Cage and Onion sat at Onion's newly renovated property.

Just like Cage he built a dwelling underground as it was no longer safe for vampires to give the illusion of normalcy on land.

His was nice but Cage's was better.

Instead of having a fake house on top which wouldn't be lived inside like Onion's, Cage's new estate would present like a warehouse, while underneath would lead to an elaborate and luxurious world fitting of a roman king.

Standing by the fire Cage and Onion sipped blood.

"I can't believe you involved Norms."

Cage sipped. "We were once Norms."

"*We* weren't Norms. *I* was. You were half blood. And I didn't respect them even then." He walked away and sat on his leather chair. "But this is going to backfire."

"Shit is coming out anyway. And what we need is organization amongst the chaos before it does."

"Is there such a thing?"

Cage took his seat. "For our sake it has to be. The Elders did me a favor by attacking me. Now I don't give a fuck what happens to all of them. At the same time, I'm supposed to give the okay to kill Angelina tomorrow."

Onion's eyes widened. "You promised to talk to her once more."

"I tried. She denied me. So she must die."

"Sir, Miss Angelina's here." Onion's servant said.

He nodded. "Invite her in."

"You invited her here?" Cage glared. "Fuck is wrong with you?"

"Just once more, Cage. Please."

"Why? So you can look like the hero?"

Onion grinned.

Five seconds later, Angelina stepped inside. She was alone and was wearing a royal blue catsuit that per usual, caught her curves.

Cage sighed. "I wasn't expecting you tonight."

"Didn't your friend tell you I was coming?"

"He's no friend of mine." Cage said to her before looking at Onion who grinned. "What made you change your mind?"

"Me and my Linas were attacked."

"By who?"

By T. STYLES

"Wolves. Sent by The Elders."

Cage sighed.

"I don't know why they're attacking me. I'm not into politics. I don't care what happens to any of you."

"That doesn't rid you of your power." He paused. "Like we said, you may not be thinking about your people now," Cage said. "But you will be thinking about us later. And since you assembled the women and female Wolves, that makes you intimidating to them."

She took a deep breath. "You are someone I consider a friend." She said to Onion. "Someone who I've come to care about a lot."

Cage glared.

What was going on? Why was she all of a sudden drawn to Onion?

"So despite disliking you, Cage, for now I'll say yes because of Onion." She looked between them both. "Tell me your plan. I want to know every fucking detail. Locations too. And I'll join you to take The Elders out. After that I'm done."

CHAPTER THIRTY-ONE
CAGE

Cage and Helena sat in their bedroom...

As she helped him dress she stared at him from the mirror. Kissing his neck, she massaged his crotch until the print of his long dick formed before her eyes. She wanted to see if he still responded to her touch. For the moment he did.

"I know what you're doing." She whispered.

He looked at her beautiful face from the mirror. "You mean saving us from The Elders?"

"No. Getting closer to Angelina."

He shook his head and walked away, before sitting on the edge of the bed. "I don't know what you're-."

"What is it about her? Why must you have her as your own?"

"I'm not interested in her. And even if I was, she claims she doesn't remember me anymore."

"Even if you *were*? So if she remembered you, would you give her a chance?"

"You know what I mean."

"No, I don't."

"What do you want me to say? You knew after Tino died it would be my responsibility to rule."

"And I want you to."

"Well she is a part of The Collective."

"But not *your* Collection. There's a difference."

"This is why I don't bother you with things like this. You get too shaken. And when you shake you–."

"Turn you off."

"Exactly. So if you know it, why you do it?"

"I will have a voice. Even if you are my king."

"And I want you to have a voice. But it doesn't mean you have to use it all the time."

Cage took a deep breath. The one thing that being with Helena forced him to do was think clearly about how he handled women. He never got over how 'weak' his mother appeared at times where he felt she should be stronger. And so he despised women who weren't go-getters. At the same time when they were too strong minded like Helena, it also turned him off.

With Angelina there was a middle ground.

But he fucked that up.

"I can't do this right now, Helena. I have to convince a group of men who have no love for me really, to help me." He walked toward the door.

"Cage."

He stopped and turned around. "Yes."

"You got this. And despite what you say, many Wolves have respect for you. And I'm so proud that my king is *the* king." She kissed him softly. "Go show them how to rule."

He nodded and walked out.

Cage prepared a major feast for his guests. The Wolves, helmed by Tatum, Row, Shannon and Canelo partook of the hefty meal he prepared.

"So, I trust that everything is cool with Flow," Cage asked, sipping on blood. He long since gave up fake eating as it did nothing for him like other vampires.

Tatum wiped his mouth after eating the most delicious raw beef he'd ever had in his life. "It hasn't been good."

Cage frowned. "Why?"

"He hasn't been around." Row said.

He shrugged. "Why…why not?"

"I'm not sure, but I think he has problems with me being in charge." Tatum responded.

By T. STYLES

Row looked away while Canelo shook his head.

"What about Bloom?"

"She's gotten up with a group of women with the sole focus of…"

"Of what?" Cage said, trying to get Tatum to finish his sentence.

"Let's discuss what we came here to discuss." Row interrupted.

"I want an answer first," Cage said firmly. "What is Bloom focusing on?"

Tatum looked at his uncles and back at his brother. "Her focus is on living up to the calling she believes Wolves have. Of killing vampires."

He shook his head. "Wow. I thought you would watch them both."

"We tried." Row said. "And we're still trying now." He paused. "But you have more information don't you, Cage?" Tatum continued. "Row and my uncles are limited, but you know exactly what's going on don't you? With these cravings? With us?"

Cage wanted to tell them everything. But with this news he feared it would be justification to kill his new family. At the same time, he was done lying. Within a matter of months, Wolves would no longer be able to deny the urge.

Something whispered in him...TELL THE TRUTH.

And so he told them all he knew.

Despite being shocked, there appeared to be a sense of relief that took over their faces. It meant not only that Bloom was right, but also that they had a responsibility to facilitate the process to prevent more people from getting hurt than need be.

"So what do you think will happen?" Tatum asked.

"The agreement we have with each other goes back longer than any of us really know." Cage paused. "We know it's time when The Cravings get undeniable. So we, the Vamps, must honor it. We must surrender."

"I'm listening, brother."

"Bloom is correct. Wolves are here to prevent vampires from overpopulating. Now it's time to reduce our numbers, which is sparked by The Cravings. As the king, I will facilitate the selection of a percentage for my people. And it will start with those who should have been chosen a long time ago. But I need the Wolves to resist if they are not meant to be a part of the battle of The Fringale. No eating us in the streets. Our homes. Shit like that."

Tatum took a deep breath. "That will be hard. To smell flesh and not take it."

"I know. Imagine how I feel. My people must die. Your people get to feast."

Tatum looked down. "The Elders you speak about, they won't go of their own accord. You said it yourself that...that they have been fighting for thousands of years."

"It doesn't make their stance right."

"So what do you want us to do?"

"There are two members in particular who are causing problems. They're Viking, who's already gone and Marco. I need Marco gone. Afterwards I will host a lottery to select the vampires who will show up for the battle. It's an old archaic way but it works."

"And we should do the same." Tatum said. "Choose who will be there."

"Exactly. The tickets you provide for the battle will be coveted by the packs, but in the end, things should die off as far as our hate for one another."

"Unless." Cheddar said.

"Unless what?" Tatum asked.

"Wolves continue to crave us after the battle."

"I spoke to Anderson." Cage stated. "And he said that after the battle there is a period of the return. It will take a moment to get back to normal, but The Cravings will subside."

They nodded.

"So what do you need now?" Tatum asked.

"Get Marco tonight."

"But it's a full moon," Tatum said. "If we target them now we could risk death."

"I know. And unfortunately we have no choice. You all have superhero strength. And so I trust your Wolves are strong enough not to get hurt. Oh, Angelina and her Minks will meet you there."

"What the fuck?" Tatum stated.

CHAPTER THIRTY-TWO
THE ELDERS

There was a blood feast taking place…

And they were drinking from the source.

The Elders, eight total, had decided that it was time to enjoy the peace of the moment. Because soon, very soon, the battle at The Fringale would begin. And although they were certain that they could find someone else to lead the younger vampires to their death, instead of themselves, they weren't entirely sure *who* anymore.

With a handsome man who was willing and ready to be bit sitting on the table, Marco looked out amongst the others and smiled. His mouth was wet with blood. "Tonight we won't worry about the future. We have given it too much time anyway."

"I agree!" One yelled.

"There's too much life to live," hollered another.

"Cage, in his insolence, continues to avoid death." Marco continued, as the smell from the man on his table had grown so strong, he stiffened in his pants. "But we'll get to him."

"He doesn't know who we are!" Danny said arrogantly. "But we will show him!"

"Exactly!"

"He believes he controls us when we are the ones who make the decisions. We are the ones who decide the direction of The Collective. And he will come to realize that he should have never crossed us."

"In Viking's name!" Someone cheered.

"And Arabia too!"

"Let's drink!" Marco laughed, eager to get to the feast below them. "Tonight we will–."

Suddenly Angelina slithered into the room, with Mink on her left and Carmen on her right. They had successfully fended off the battle on the racetrack, and now they entered the vampire premises thirty deep.

"Hello, Gentleman," she said as she stood next to Marco at the head of the table. Per usual she wore her outfit of choice, an all-white lace catsuit. "I take it I'm not interrupting anything of value."

The Wolves moved to the right of the table in pack formation.

Her vampires moved to the left.

The Elders were stronger than most Vamps and Wolves. The trouble is, they were outnumbered.

"Who are you?" Marco yelled through clenched teeth.

"You know exactly who my queen is," Carmen responded.

"Because you tried to kill her," Mink added. "Many times!"

"We didn't try to kill anyone!" Marco lied, his body trembling with fear at how the Wolves looked at him. "We were simply trying to get the younger vampires to understand that–."

"We don't need to understand!" Angelina continued. "We need to be left alone. But you couldn't do that!"

"That's where you're wrong!" Marco continued. "Your actions have caused all of us great distress. Literally the rise of your Linas has brought attention to vampires in the public eye. And if we are made known, we run the risk of being captured by the authorities, locked in prison, and dying due to being exposed to sunlight."

"No one will ever capture me." Angelina promised. "I can't say the same for you."

"You're arrogant but beautiful!" Marco said. "And that's what makes you dangerous. That's what has caused us problems."

"You should've left me out of your war." She said calmly. "Now it's too late." She looked at her team. "Feast!"

The Wolves jumped on top of The Elders as they struggled to get away. Although the older vampires were very strong, The Cravings gave the Wolves strength and power they didn't have access to in the past.

Whenever an Elder attempted to make an exit, a Lina would toss him back into the center where a Wolf would do the rest. Through the melee, The Norms, who were there for The Elders, were suckled by Angelina's vampires.

In the end, Angelina had taken out most of the leadership of The Elders in Maryland except for three who once again escaped underground.

And unfortunately, as planned, Cage's Wolves, led by Tatum which included Row, Canelo, and Shannon, showed up to the scene per the scheduled time.

"What's this?" Tatum asked, confused at what he was seeing.

Angelina smiled. "We took out The Elders. What does it look like?"

By T. STYLES

"But we were supposed to be working together." Tatum said, looking around. "Cage said you were with part two of the plan."

Angelina wiped the blood off her mouth. Climbing on top of the table barefoot, she stared down at them. "Why did he think I would allow him to control me? I wanted the details of his plan so I can do shit myself. Fuck Cage! Fuck Onion too!"

Tatum glared.

"He doesn't own me!" She walked around the carcasses of The Elders that the Minks feasted upon. "He doesn't own my Linas either. And if Cage has a problem with it, you tell him to come see me."

CHAPTER THIRTY-THREE
CAGE

Cage paced the floor in rage upon hearing what Tatum and Row said about Angelina, her Linas, and the Minks.

"She…she went ahead of your Wolves and fucked shit up!" Cage yelled. Langley stood toward the right, Helena to the left. "How could she do that? She fucking let three of them niggas get away!"

"I know…I know." Tatum said. "But the way they did it, the way they devoured The Elders felt personal."

Cage paused. "Explain."

"You know her better than me but–."

"What do you mean, brother?"

"She seems to be fighting some inner demons, Cage." Tatum said seriously. "Some inner pain. What happened to her when she was your wife?"

Silence.

"Cage, what happened?"

"Too much to say and too little time."

"I know we aren't meant to get along." Tatum said, stepping forward. "But you're still my brother. I think

By T. STYLES

she's coming for you next. So let me say this, you should hit her first. While you still can."

Cage took a deep breath and nodded.

3 MONTHS LATER
THE LOTTERY

The theater was packed, once again with the leaders of the largest Collections in each state throughout the United States and abroad.

This private event was televised.

To be present, Cage solicited the leaders of the biggest Collections in every country around the world. It took a while; most flew on jets chartered in the middle of the night. But after some time they were there. And they were ready for the truth.

Many things had happened since they last saw him. He no longer shuttered from being king. He realized that unless he stepped into his rightful position, everything, and everybody he loved would fall.

Including the son he had yet to meet.

There was no more time for games.

A percentage would be selected for the battle that night.

First he told them the truth.

The secret which had been held from younger vampires around the world for hundreds of years. He bombarded them with the details they needed to know. That their existence, the very reason they breathed was to push humanity to the brink of death so that they could learn who they truly were...

Precious Beings.

They grunted upon learning of their purpose, but it wasn't hard to believe. Besides, Wolves in every place in the world had awakened and started craving their flesh over the past few years. Many knew there was a reason and now they were hearing the truth for the first time.

"So basically, them old ass bitches lied to us!" A Crenshaw vampire yelled. "I knew I ain't trust them niggas!"

More chatter amongst The Collective.

When they settled down, he took a deep breath. "And now it's time for the hardest part of the night. But I can't hope that we will be able to assemble in enough time for the fight. So it has to be now." He paused. "I have in this chest, the leaders in each city, state, and country throughout the world. When I pull the name,

274   By T. STYLES

each of you is responsible for delivering four of your eldest vampires here, for the battle of The Fringale."

"But how?" A leader from Chicago yelled.

"That's up to you. But as of today, this is law. And if you don't run your cities, states, and countries by delivering your elders who have lived their share of time, I will bring the Wolves to you personally."

Outrage stirred the crowd.

"And how do you intend on doing that, my nigga?"

Cage looked behind him and nodded. Suddenly Tatum stepped from the back and stood at his side.

His pack growled in the background.

Tatum raised his hand silencing his people who grew uneasy in the audience.

Cage did the same.

"I told you he was a wolf lover," a Utah vampire yelled. "Who turns Wolves on their own people?"

He was immediately struck in the face by an Arizona Vamp who respected Cage. The Mag, armed vampires with guns laced with D, prepared for more melee. The guards covered each aisle and every one of them prepared to release the poison on Cage's word.

"I am not my father!" Cage yelled to the vampires. "There will be order in this mothafucka or I will chop each one of you down I swear to God!"

The room settled.

"The percentage must happen!" Cage continued. "We have no choice. Plus let's keep it one hundred. Them niggas lived long enough already! Let us young boys have our day!"

Utah's leader shifted with rage. Despite being bruised by the blow and healing instantly.

"It is now that you must get control of your people. Or we all die! Is that what you want?"

Silence.

Cage took a deep breath and placed himself in their shoes. "Prior to taking The Fluid, many of us would only live sixty to seventy years as a Norm. Some less than that. Being Vamp affords you hundreds of years. Why do you want to live longer than this anyway? To see loved ones perish and die? To long for the sun, while being forced to settle for the moon."

Light chatter.

"The lottery will happen and you will respect my word or I'll murder you niggas right now. Fuck is it gonna be?"

The guards aimed.

Utah nodded in solidarity.

Cage looked back. "Come, brother."

Tatum stepped up. "We...all of us...are species of the night. I don't know why God made us this way but here we are. As a result, I have spoken to the packs worldwide. They have agreed to fall back. But if you don't honor this new law, that my brother has laid out, I will have no other choice but to release the packs into your streets. Into your homes. Into your nightclubs. The battle of The Fringale will happen here, or it will happen in your countries, cities, states, or your front porches."

Cage placed a hand on his shoulder. Walking over to the large glass case he said, "Shall the lottery begin?"

Anderson said goodbye to his family members weeks ago...

He was excited and ready to be chosen for the battle of The Fringale in a few weeks. But his number had yet to be called as he watched the televised event. What was happening?

KNOCK. KNOCK. KNOCK.

He stood up and opened the door. On the other side was Cage and Tatum. He recognized them and let them both in.

"I'm ready to go to the battle. Where do I report?"

"I need you right now. I can't let you report to the battle. I'm sorry."

He frowned. "What...but...but that's dishonorable. You promised!"

"Listen, my father is gone. As you know. And you are a wealth of information. I'm not ready to part with that yet. Especially after losing Arabia and Viking. But if you give me some more time. I-."

"This is wrong."

"Yes, it's true. But kings have to make tough decisions. And so I'm making tough decisions now." He looked back at his brother. "But when you want to die, my brother here is sure to do the job."

Anderson took a deep breath and lowered his head. "To die at The Fringale is with honor. To die like you are a piece of meat is not something I want to subject myself to. I beg you to reconsider."

"I did reconsider. I reconsidered your request to go to The Fringale. And my answer is still no."

CHAPTER THIRTY-FOUR
FLOW

Flow and Gunnar were walking in the woods as the sun set high in the sky. More Wolves who still pledged allegiance to Flow, mostly outcasts of course, followed from behind.

"I can't believe Tatum is still loyal to Cage." Gunnar said. "And yet they still allow him to sit on the throne. To run the packs as if we're property."

"When you think about it, it makes sense for Tatum. They're literally handing over meals to the Wolves. If anybody is unbenefited, it's Cage. And I just have to find a vampire who hates him just as much as we do. Maybe they'll finally rise up against him."

"Still hate your brother?" Gunnar laughed.

"The nigga still hates me." He paused. "But yes."

Suddenly they walked into the open field where a small cottage stood on a patch of grass. It wasn't modern at all. Something out of a story book, but it certainly didn't look out of place.

"I told you it was here," Gunnar said proudly.

"You did good," Flow responded with a grin.

The Minks in all their beauty ran, played, and jumped around the cottage, enjoying their lives. That is until she saw him.

The moment Mink spotted the love of her life, her heartbeat heavily in her chest. She couldn't believe her eyes. From a distance she said, "F...Flow?"

He looked back at Gunnar and the other Wolves. "Stay here."

"You sure?"

He nodded yes.

Uncertain of what was happening, beautiful female Wolves walked behind her for protection, but it was Mink who was almost brought to her knees.

"Flow..." her fingers covered her lips as she stepped away from her women. "Is that...is that you?"

He pulled her closely as she wept in his arms. So much time had passed since she last saw him. And she was literally weakened in the knees.

"You...you are so fine," he said.

She touched her face and hips. "Re...really? My queen has been taking care of me."

"Your queen huh?" He glared. "I see."

The moment he stood in her presence, he wanted to be inside of her. How she stood up against the packs and rolled with Angelina by forming her own crew was sexy as fuck. Besides, she had done it in his name.

But he was home now.

To catch up, he told her everything that happened. How Cage grew worried about Bloom, with her cravings, would start a war and so he locked them both away.

Mink told him about her travels…about how many Wolves followed her lead. And how much she loved and respected Angelina.

"Angelina." He said with a smile. "You know we can't let her continue to grow to more power right? You know you can't allow yourself to be ruled by her anymore? I heard about how she led Cage and Onion's men to kill your girls. You gonna let that shit slide?"

She looked behind her and stepped further away from her Wolves. "You can't talk about her like that." She whispered. "You don't understand what happened."

"She's not our people!" He said through clenched teeth. "She's not one of us."

"Flow…what are you…what are you saying?" She smiled. "She was the person who gave me a place to go when the pack isolated me. When they-."

"I want you to come away with me. Let me be that person now."

She nodded. "I want nothing more."

"Then where is she? Show her to me and I'll believe you." Suddenly his Wolves exited the woods and stood behind him. Rubbing her arms he said, "Where is Angelina?"

"Why would I need to show you my queen to–."

"She is not your fucking queen! Now you are my woman! You belong to me! Where is that bitch?"

"What are you…what are you doing?" She was trembling. "Why did you bring all of these Wolves to–."

"If I hand her over, the Wolves in the pack will respect me more." Flow said. "And I can regain the throne. But I need her body. I need you."

Mink's heart beat fast.

Angelina was hidden in a special place that only she knew about under the cottage. The Day Walkers Carmen hired, would've provided assistance against Flow but they weren't there yet. No one expected this attack. And so she was handling this alone.

Flow pressed harder, kissing her lips, and running his hand between her legs. She was wet the moment he laid eyes on her. "Come on, baby. I don't wanna fight with you. Where is she? Where does she rest? Let us eat her flesh. Together."

Mink trembled as tears rolled down her cheeks. "I...I can't do that. I'm sorry."

He glared. "What do you mean you can't do that? I am your–."

She howled, assembling all Wolves on sight.

Just that quickly a fight ensued. Each man and woman with wolf blood coursing through their veins took up arms.

That included both Flow and Mink.

Blow after blow.

Bite after bite.

In the end Flow and Gunnar's men overpowered the Minks as each one suffered a blow to the neck, one of the fewest ways to kill Wolves. They fought their hardest. They fought with love. They fought with honor. The Wolf nation would have to reconsider how they handled their women who for one reason or another ended up manless, that was for sure.

Because the Minks found a sisterhood that transcended their species.

And they gave their lives.

Lying on the ground, weakened but not dead, Mink looked up at Flow.

"This type of loyalty is sexy. But it should've been focused on me. That's why you must die."

He popped her neck.

With no time left to heal, due to the injury, he watched life drift from her eyes.

Mink, and many of her Wolves, had fallen.

But never folded.

And so Angelina remained alive.

CHAPTER THIRTY-FIVE
CAGE

Cage and Onion sat in the most elite vampire club in the states which was owned by Cage. After the lottery was completed, they had to wait on the leaders in each state to hand over their Elders.

"You think it'll go down as planned?" Onion asked.

Cage sighed. "For their sake it better."

"So what about the Maryland Elders? Since you the boss, are you going to make sure they report to the battle?"

"We took care of most of them. But the ones who are still alive, I will find them, and they will do their duty."

"Will you really unleash the Wolves everywhere else? Or was that just a threat? Because if you do, you will be the enemy to your own people."

"I'm the enemy already."

"With some of The Elders, yes. However, many of them understand. Got tired of living each century and seeing no change. But if you release the Wolves in places that don't turn over The Elders...well...you never know."

"I can't worry about that anymore." Cage paused. "But I finally know why you wanted me to be at odds with Angelina. And target her, her Linas and her Wolves."

"What you talking 'bout?"

"The angrier she got with me, the easier it would be for her to love you."

Onion's jaw dropped but he closed his mouth. "Not true. I-."

"I'm on to you. And I decided to write my own ending to my story. You won't be able to-."

Suddenly Angelina walked into the club.

Unlike in the past, this time she was alone.

Slowly Cage rose. "What are you doing here? You aren't-."

"They killed them." She said walking up to him.

Onion rose too.

"Killed who?" Cage said.

"Mink. We woke up and she was...gone. All of them."

Onion nodded, realizing she had finally come home.

Stepping up to her, Onion said, "Don't worry about it, I will take care of you. I will make sure you and your Linas are safe."

"She doesn't need you," Cage said. "She's been doing this on her own for the longest."

Angelina looked up at Onion and said, "No, I do need Onion. I finally realized that I should have been with him all along. So I pledge my..."

Suddenly her words seemed lost.

As if missing in the ether.

When Cage tried to speak the same thing happened. He couldn't. He tried several times to open his mouth and talk but nothing.

It was as if they were being taken from their world leaving...........................

Only...

....

....

....

Space..

....

PRESENT DAY

Pierre and Violet looked in awe as Kehinde continued to delete chapters from the novel on the computer.

"Why did you do that?" Violet said, holding her belly and lips. "Why delete that entire section. We...had done so much."

"It just didn't make sense," Kehinde responded. "Angelina not remembering the character Cage." He gave Pierre a sly look. "Her wanting to be with Onion all of a sudden. It's all off."

"What about the meeting with The Elders?" She spoke.

"I think that is great." Kehinde nodded. "Which is why it will remain while other parts won't."

"Don't worry," Pierre looked back at Violet. "I have another file saved. If you like what we did together that much we can put it back."

Kehinde jumped up and faced Pierre. "Why is that version so important?"

"Which part? The lottery? The beef with The Elders?"

"No...Angelina forgetting Cage." Kehinde glared. "Why is that so important to you? Are you trying to live

288   By T. STYLES

vicariously through the Onion character? Because the woman never wanted you on the page, so you have to force her to want you in life?"

Violet stood by and waited for an answer.

"Because in my mind, she always loved Onion." Pierre continued. "So shouldn't they be together?"

"She made her decision that they could only be friends years ago!" Cage yelled. "In the beginning of the series. When they were fucking kids!"

"Wait, we are talking about characters right," Violet interrupted. "Remember, these people, these...these vampires aren't real."

Kehinde and Pierre looked at one another, both breathing heavily.

Kehinde dragged his hand down his face and focused back on Pierre. "All I'm saying is that Violet's grandmother wrote these characters the way that she did because...because she wanted them to be together. Cage and Angelina. And messing with that is a disservice."

"None of it will matter anyway." Violet whispered.

They focused on her again.

"Why?" Pierre asked.

"Because Abuela didn't make a lot clear about the direction she wanted me to take with the ending. Except for...except for the fact that she wanted death to all vampires and Wolves in her books. Because she was afraid–."

"Afraid of what?" Kehinde said.

"That leaving them alive...or leaving the series without an end, would leave them free to move upon our world." She paused. "The real world."

Kehinde and Pierre stared at each other in horror. Prior to this moment, Pierre was only interested in finally getting the love of his life. And now he was learning he would have no life.

Kehinde, was realizing the same thing too.

"So, so, she wants to kill us?" Kehinde said.

"Kill us?" She said softly, slightly afraid.

"I'm sorry...I mean, kill Cage?"

"And Onion too?" Pierre interjected.

"Yes." Her eyes widened. "Why...why are you both so afraid?"

The silence was deafening and then...

RING. RING.

"Expecting a call?" Pierre asked when he heard Violet's home phone.

"No." She walked toward it. Picking up the red handle she said, "Hello." Her eyes remained on them both. And their eyes remained on her.

Suddenly she was quite afraid as they moved nearer.

She looked down, to avoid their stares. Slowly her head rose, and the fear was replaced with a huge smile that burst into crying laughter. "Are you...are you serious?" Pure joy spread across her cheeks.

Silence.

"Yes, yes! Right away." She placed down the handset.

"What is it?" Pierre asked.

"That was my Abuela! She's...she's awake! And she wants me to come to her now. With a pen and a pad! She said she's going to finish her own book before she dies!"

Pierre and Kehinde dragged their hands down their faces.

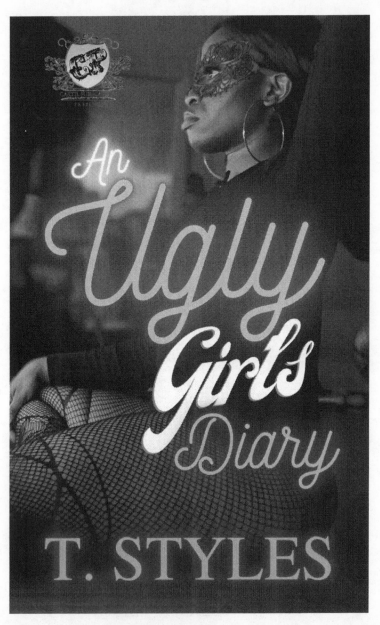

An Ugly Girl's Diary

T. STYLES

By T. STYLES

CARTEL PUBLICATIONS

PRESENTS

The Cartel Publications Order Form

www.thecartelpublications.com

Inmates **ONLY** receive novels for $12.00 per book **PLUS** shipping fee **PER BOOK.**

(Mail Order **MUST** come from inmate directly to receive discount)

Shyt List 1	_____	$15.00
Shyt List 2	_____	$15.00
Shyt List 3	_____	$15.00
Shyt List 4	_____	$15.00
Shyt List 5	_____	$15.00
Shyt List 6	_____	$15.00
Pitbulls In A Skirt	_____	$15.00
Pitbulls In A Skirt 2	_____	$15.00
Pitbulls In A Skirt 3	_____	$15.00
Pitbulls In A Skirt 4	_____	$15.00
Pitbulls In A Skirt 5	_____	$15.00
Victoria's Secret	_____	$15.00
Poison 1	_____	$15.00
Poison 2	_____	$15.00
Hell Razor Honeys	_____	$15.00
Hell Razor Honeys 2	_____	$15.00
A Hustler's Son	_____	$15.00
A Hustler's Son 2	_____	$15.00
Black and Ugly	_____	$15.00
Black and Ugly As Ever	_____	$15.00
Ms Wayne & The Queens of DC **(LGBTQ)**	_____	$15.00
Black And The Ugliest	_____	$15.00
Year Of The Crackmom	_____	$15.00
Deadheads	_____	$15.00
The Face That Launched A Thousand Bullets	_____	$15.00
The Unusual Suspects	_____	$15.00
Paid In Blood	_____	$15.00
Raunchy	_____	$15.00
Raunchy 2	_____	$15.00
Raunchy 3	_____	$15.00
Mad Maxxx (4th Book Raunchy Series)	_____	$15.00
Quita's Dayscare Center	_____	$15.00
Quita's Dayscare Center 2	_____	$15.00
Pretty Kings	_____	$15.00
Pretty Kings 2	_____	$15.00
Pretty Kings 3	_____	$15.00
Pretty Kings 4	_____	$15.00

TREASON 3

Silence Of The Nine _____	$15.00
Silence Of The Nine 2 _____	$15.00
Silence Of The Nine 3 _____	$15.00
Prison Throne _____	$15.00
Drunk & Hot Girls _____	$15.00
Hersband Material **(LGBTQ)** _ _____	$15.00
The End: How To Write A _____	$15.00
Bestselling Novel In 30 Days (Non-Fiction Guide)	
Upscale Kittens _____	$15.00
Wake & Bake Boys _____	$15.00
Young & Dumb _____	$15.00
Young & Dumb 2: Vyce's Getback _____	$15.00
Tranny 911 **(LGBTQ)** _____	$15.00
Tranny 911: Dixie's Rise **(LGBTQ)** _____	
$15.00	
First Comes Love, Then Comes Murder _____	$15.00
Luxury Tax _____	$15.00
The Lying King _____	$15.00
Crazy Kind Of Love _____	$15.00
Goon _____	$15.00
And They Call Me God _____	$15.00
The Ungrateful Bastards _____	$15.00
Lipstick Dom **(LGBTQ)** _____	$15.00
A School of Dolls **(LGBTQ)** _____	$15.00
Hoetic Justice _____	$15.00
KALI: Raunchy Relived _____	$15.00
(5th Book in Raunchy Series)	
Skeezers _____	$15.00
Skeezers 2 _____	$15.00
You Kissed Me, Now I Own You _____	$15.00
Nefarious _____	$15.00
Redbone 3: The Rise of The Fold _____	$15.00
The Fold (4th Redbone Book) _____	$15.00
Clown Niggas _____	$15.00
The One You Shouldn't Trust _____	$15.00
The WHORE The Wind	
Blew My Way _____	$15.00
She Brings The Worst Kind _____	$15.00
The House That Crack Built _____	$15.00
The House That Crack Built 2 _____	15.00
The House That Crack Built 3 _____	$15.00
The House That Crack Built 4 _____	$15.00
Level Up **(LGBTQ)** _____	$15.00
Villains: It's Savage Season _____	$15.00
Gay For My Bae _____	$15.00
War _____	$15.00
War 2: All Hell Breaks Loose _____	$15.00
War 3: The Land Of The Lou's _____	$15.00
War 4: Skull Island _____	$15.00
War 5: Karma _____	$15.00
War 6: Envy _____	$15.00
War 7: Pink Cotton _____	$15.00
Madjesty vs. Jayden (Novella) _____	$8.99
You Left Me No Choice _____	$15.00
Truce – A War Saga (War 8) _____	$15.00
Ask The Streets For Mercy _____	$15.00
Truce 2 (War 9) _____	$15.00
An Ace and Walid Very, Very Bad Christmas (War 10) _____	$15.00
Truce 3 – The Sins of The Fathers (War 11) _____	$15.00
Truce 4: The Finale (War 12) _____	$15.00
Treason _____	$20.00
Treason 2 _____	$20.00

Hersband Material 2 **(LGBTQ)** _____ $15.00
The Gods Of Everything Else (War 13) _____ $15.00
The Gods Of Everything Else 2 (War 14) _____ $15.00
Treason 3 _____ $15.99

(**Redbone 1** & **2** are **NOT** Cartel Publications novels and if <u>ordered</u> the cost is **FULL** price of $16.00 **each plus shipping**. <u>No Exceptions</u>.)

Please add **$7.00** for shipping and handling fees for up to **(2) BOOKS PER ORDER**. (INMATES INCLUDED) (See next page for details)

The Cartel Publications * P.O. BOX 486 OWINGS MILLS MD 21117

Name: _____

Address: _____

City/State: _____

Contact/Email: _____

Please allow 10-15 BUSINESS days Before shipping.

PLEASE NOTE DUE TO <u>COVID-19</u> SOME ORDERS MAY TAKE UP TO <u>3 WEEKS</u> <u>OR LONGER</u> BEFORE THEY SHIP

The Cartel Publications is <u>NOT</u> responsible for <u>Prison Orders</u> rejected!

<u>NO RETURNS and NO REFUNDS</u>
<u>NO PERSONAL CHECKS ACCEPTED</u>
<u>STAMPS NO LONGER ACCEPTED</u>

Made in the USA
Columbia, SC
02 June 2022

61254845R00176